WHEN THE STUGGLE GETS REAL

Priscilla Evans

DEDICATION

First of all, I would like to give all praises to the Most High God Almighty. Life hasn't been easy, but there has always been a still small voice that carried me through. A special acknowledgment to my children, sisters, brothers, nieces, nephews, and my "Mama", aka Frankie Mae Walker **RIP.** Doors have been opening for us. To all the people who didn't believe in me, it never mattered anyway. I knew God had His hands on me all along. Last but not least, thanks to all of my fans! I'm on my way to the top! Writing has become a new hobby for me; I love it!

TABLE OF CONTENTS

PREFACE

Just because things may appear to be good on the outside, God only knows the pain that's on the inside. Strength is deep within. Each day I fight to live. I'll never give up on what I believe in. No, it hasn't been an easy road to travel, but there's always sun after the storm. I'm determined there's no stopping. Welcome to a world of many struggles.

INTRODUCTION

Who is Janikkia Jones, aka, Nikki? Well, to be honest, I'm still trying to figure that out. One thing is for sure, I have gone through a lot in life, and I am still here. As we speak, I'm going through yet another transition in my life. You know my mama always told me that if you haven't gone through any struggles in your life, keep living. I for damn sure have had my share of struggles, many of which I was born into. But it's because of Mama, my guardian angel and God, that I have made it this far.

Not so long ago, I was asked by my life coach what I would like for my obituary to say about me when I die. This question was difficult to answer, and I still don't quite have it all figured out, yet. But what I can say for now is that I want people to be able to say, I didn't quit. I've learned through prayer, meditation, and spending time with God, that God has a way of using our pain for a purpose. Even in the midst of my struggles, God has always been right there with me. As I look around my surroundings at the moment, all I see are women who grew up a lot like me. We have endured abuse and neglect, witnessed and experienced domestic violence, and lost sight of who we are. Hell, to be honest, I, for one, have never really known my identity. It took this and being still for me to truly find my true self and learn that I do not have to be a product of my environment. I can change and be a better woman.

That said, I am going to take you with me back in time, on my journey. My journey has been full of twists and turns and my struggles have gotten really real.

CHAPTER ONE

Today has been a very good one. Mama is at it again, in the kitchen, hooking the soul food up. She has the house stankin, and it smells good as hell. Mom is cooking fried pork chops, homemade macaroni and cheese, collard greens, and corn. Nikki thinks to herself, "being that she worked all day long at a sewing plant for many years, in spite of it all, she's still holding down a family of eight." Everybody from the baby boy to the oldest girl was watching T.V. Nikki noticed her dad's truck pulling up in the driveway. How could I not notice it, for real? Daddy's truck was loud with a light blue tent. Our family has taken many trips to Lake Oconee in that same truck.

Excited to see dad enter the living room door, I jumped for joy at the sight of a new toy. I've always been the center of attention in daddy's eyes, "Daddy's little shining star", as he would always say.

All along, what I thought was the perfect family, laid so many hidden secrets. 10:30 p.m., and I'm startled out of sleep by screaming. Scared and confused at the same time, I could hear mom yelling. "Please, please, David, don't hit me again!'. I was so afraid and scared of the unknown, really not understanding what was taking place behind the doors of my parent's room.

Jumping out of bed, my alarm clock read 1:30 a.m. I peep down the long dark hallway of our four-bedroom apartment. Mom comes rushing out of her room, and he's behind her. Mom and daddy noticed that I was watching, so they both pretended that everything was just fine. "Please don't be mean to mama." I whisper to no one in particular.

Sadness has come over a home that was once filled with happiness. Mom told me to go back to bed because I had school tomorrow. Just like always, she was trying to make everything alright. Doing what I was told to do, I lay in my twin size bed and I felt hate from inside my guts. No, I didn't in any way like my father's actions. Headed to the restroom that sits right across the hall of my bedroom, stopping right in my tracks, I notice that mom was lying on the couch and the door to the room that my parents shared was closed.

Why, why, why does all of this seem to be happening to the most amazing woman I've ever known? "Mama?" I whisper, now realizing she couldn't hear a word. I approach the couch. Tears are falling. "You can sleep with me mama. I'll keep you safe." Who in this world would think a ten-year-old girl would feel as if she needs to protect her mother from harm? Isn't it supposed to be the other way around? Welcome to the very first night of my life. It made a major turn for the worse.

"Nikki what's the answer to this math problem?" My teacher, Ms. Walker asked, catching me off guard.

"Damn!" is all I could say. I wasn't paying any attention while she was teaching. My mind was still on the other night and what happened with my parents. Sitting in class was the last thing I wanted to do. I noticed that my classmates were looking in my direction.

Ms. Walker said, "I knew you were slow, Nikki." The class laughed at me. Before I knew it, I was up out of my seat. "SLAP! SLAP!" I hit Stacy. Mad and ready for whatever at this point. I hit his ass a third time.

"Nikki! Step out in the hall!" yelled Ms. Walker.

"What's up, Ms. Walker?"

"You can't just be slapping people and think that it's okay," said Ms. Walker

"Whatever," I said as I pushed past her. "Go to the principal's office!"

Now realizing mama's old saying, "There are consequences behind every action."

"Now, what am I going to do?" I thought to myself. "I'm suspended for three days."

Back at it and it's another day. As soon as my feet hit Carol High School, "Stop right there!" Principal Simpson instructed me, "to my office! Now Nikki, you were told that you have been suspended, which means you were not supposed to be here today."

"Please, Mr. Simpson! Don't call my parents! I'll get into more trouble." Not caring about my plea to him, Mr. Simpson called anyway.

"Hello Mr. Davis, I need you to come by the school to pick your daughter up." Mr. Simpson said sternly on the phone and then hung up. That was the very first day I had been abused and spoken to as if l was dumb.

"Look at you! You'll never be anything!" Dad yelled in my direction in a very stem tone of voice that made me fear him. I believed everything that he said I was. The hate I was feeling only increased toward him. I'd been introduced to hate and for some reason, it was growing stronger. The man that I once loved and thought the world of, I now despised with every part of my being that I had inside of my soul.

It's later in the day and the middle of June. All the kids in the hood are outdoors, enjoying the weather.

"Hey Nikki, get in here and fix me something to drink!" Daddy yelled like always.

"Huh." I thought to myself, "You bastard I have something for you." An idea came to mind that I got from one of my favorite movies, "Color Purple". I discovered a new trick for his ass.

"I'll be glad to fix you something." I spit right in his cup.

Standing in the kitchen corner, a sudden rush came over me, and I got excited that daddy was drinking my spit. "He deserves it," I stated to myself. I don't know why, but at that moment I thought about my mom. No matter what, she never allowed what took place in her life to affect her motherhood. Mom was the BEST!

CHAPTER TWO

As I was becoming a teenager, I wanted to fit in. I wanted to feel needed and wanted at the same time, reaching out to people twice my age. People outside of our family became a comfort to me. I was sitting under the big oak tree in the front yard at the age of thirteen. Blown by what I saw, "Who is that?" I stated to the air and to no one in particular, but myself. He looked in my direction before going out the back door that was in front of mine.

"Damn!" as I thought, "nice house for it to stay full of hood niggas. I want to be a part of that." That thought didn't last long because I dismissed it quickly.

"Nikki, get in this damn house! Why aren't those dishes washed yet?" David yelled.

"O God, this man makes me sick, for real! Why did he have to be my father?" I thought to myself.

"And you better stop looking like that before I slap those eyes in the back of your head!" Dad said. I just couldn't understand why he had to be so rude and mean to us.

Washing up the last of the dishes he had in the sink, I noticed David giving himself a shot of something with a needle and a

little clear bottle he held. I later found out that he had diabetes, and he was taking his insulin shot for today.
"Dirty bitch! That's what you get." I whisper to myself.

Mama's car was pulling into the driveway. A big smile crossed my face. I love that woman, and words will never explain or compare how much I love her. The door opens.

"Hey, Mam. How was your day?

"Just fine, sweetie. I'm a little worn out; busy day. Go get the bags out of my car, Nikki."

 I didn't mind doing anything she asked of me. Mama has always been the peaceful, loving type."

Ring, ring, ring.

"Somebody should answer that fucking phone!" Daddy yelled from the living room.

"Hello? Hey, what's up, Shan?" Shan was a classmate from school.

"I've missed you too, Nikki." Shan said from the other end of the phone.

"I'll be back tomorrow," I told her.

Shan was my little partner, and we trusted each other. That day, I told my partner how scared I had become about the situation of with my dad abusing my mom.

"Shan, I feel like one day, he will hit mama the wrong way and hurt her really bad. "

She told me that everything would be just fine. In the moment I felt dismissed, so I quickly changed the subject. But deep down, I was crying out for help and needed to tell someone what was happening before something serious happened to my mom. I started to feel like the whole world was on my shoulders. No one understands, so why talk about it?

A day or two later, I was cooling in the bedroom, looking out the window. My mind was in a million places at once, which ain't nothing new. I noticed this guy named Bay, from the other day in the yard. This time he spoke to me and of course, I spoke back. My room window is half-way up.

"What's up, shorty?" Bay said.
"Shit, nothing but cooling it.". I maturely replied.
"How old are you, ma?"

Knowing that I was about to lie, "Eighteen years old," I blurted out. Hell, I looked that age anyway. What he doesn't know won't

hurt him, I thought to myself. Any attention at this point in my life is better than none. I needed it.
"Yo, you want to come over and hang out with a nigga later on?"

"Yeah, why not?", I answered.

"Cool. I have a few errands I need to run, so I'll pull up on you later at your sister's spot. You're welcome to come over."

"Check," I said calmly.

Swiftly, I started to ponder and strategize how I was gonna be able to sneak out of the house around 10:00p.m.

"The hell with it.", I thought to myself. Mom and dad should be asleep and they won't know. Things couldn't possibly get any worse than they are already, right?

"Get your lazy ass up!" yelled my dad. "Clean this nasty room up before I beat your ass, Nikki!"

"Here we go again." I said to myself. "I'm sick of his mean ass, for real! I really wish he would drop dead."

While heading back to my room with the mop and broom, I noticed a bottle of my dad's insulin sitting on the countertop. For a moment, I loss myself thinking about adding vinegar to it. Maybe it would kill him. One part of me said, "Do it." The other

part said, "You will be judged one day." I just kept walking to my room.
"Nikki?" Shaken out of my thoughts. "Yes mom?" I responded.
"Are you okay?" she asked. "Yes, I'm okay."
"I love you. Sometimes you have to overlook your dad."

For some reason, she always made up excuses for him, one way or another. Something I didn't or couldn't understand. "Yes, ma'am." I responded.

10:15 p.m. I'm shaking and shit. The thought of sneaking out of this house has me so nervous, but shit, "I'm doing it all or nothing." I said. Down the hallway to our apartment, it sounds like two adult bears in the room. That's the sound of my parents and I knew that they had to be asleep. Deep snores echo off the walls.

"Damn! That was really close." I thought finishing up with getting myself together for that day. The turn-up just got real! Sneaking out had become an every-other-night type of thing in my world. "I think I'm in love." I thought out loud.

While sitting at dinner one night, Mama blew my mind with what came from her mouth, "Nikki, I scheduled you an appointment."

"What in the hell was she talking about?" We never had a conversation about an appointment.

Just when I thought things couldn't get any worse, while sitting at the table eating one of mama's wonderful soul food meals, (Nothing could ever compare to mama and her cooking... I thought to myself while meatloaf, green beans, sweet com, and dinner rolls), mama finally dropped a bomb on me.

"So, Nikki, I'm taking you to your doctor's appointment Monday, so we can be on the safe side."

"What?" I asked, with a puzzled look on my face. What do you mean, mama?"

"Baby, I want you to be on some type of birth control, that's all."

Now that we are talking about this, I started to get this funny feeling in the pit of my belly. I think to myself, while sitting there, "I haven't had a period in three months. Why would mama want me on the pill anyway?" Mama's mother's intuition was something serious. Not able to finish the rest of my dinner I excused myself, "What just happened?" I thought. Question after question formed in my head.

Tonight, Is The Night

"Why the fuck you cut me out!" Yelled Larry from across the table from his card partner.

Sitting in a house full of grown people, I had to be the toughest one in the crowd, for real. Drinking like I belonged there. Damn, the Bud light I was drinking was so good and some kind of feeling overcame me. I felt like I had no problems in the world. I felt like grinding to the song that was playing, 'Let's get this party started right, let's get this party started quickly! Like set it off on the left y'all, set it off on the right y'all, set it off."

Unaware of another monster that I had allowed into my world, alcohol had become my get away from my worries.

"Damn I love this feeling!" I thought to myself.

I knew that I would have many more days like this. Drinking had become my new way to escape from the problems of the world.

"So little mama, let's say we get out of this crowded room so we can get to know one another better." Bay said.

"Ok, let's go," I willingly agreed.

I'm now on a second drink allowing the alcohol to flow through my young veins. Before I knew it, I was in a room with Bay having sex and not even thinking about the consequences that could come with it all. I honestly will never forget that night.

"Girls, it's time to rise and shine.", Mama said from the door of our bedroom.

Our family was big. There were three girls and five boys in our household. All three girls shared a room. Brushing my teeth and getting ready to face another day, was a struggle. Heaven, my sister, let me know that she saw me last night climbing out our window.

"Please don't tell no body," I begged of her.

"Chill, I won't. I will be on the same shit you be on, on the real", she boasted.

As I always do, I got deep into my thoughts. "Does she know that I'm having sex? Does she know I haven't had a period?" These questions went on in my head for about 20 minutes or so.

I looked across the room and noticed my oldest sister, Eve, on the telephone talking to her boyfriend. The radio was playing a slow jam by the R & B group X-scape, "Do you want to, like I want to, I want to make love to you. Say you do." John has been Eve's man since high school. Not noticing me standing there I just let her do her thing and lay on the bottom of the bed. I went to sleep and didn't even realize it.

"Nikki, get up! Get up, Nikki!"

I thought that I was just having a bad dream, but it was Eve telling me that daddy was beating mama again. I jumped straight up out of bed, heading in the direction of the sounds. I thought to myself, "Maybe, just maybe if he notices me, he will stop being so mean to mama." Damn, I really hate it when he comes in on a late night and takes his anger out on her. My thoughts were in overdrive and my heart was beating out of my chest. I could hear that mother fucker yelling.

"Bitch! I told you not to ask me where I been," dad yells while grabbing mama's neck.

"Slap! Slap! Slap!" It went on for about an hour or so. I wish I could help mama, but once again I had become a helpless child in the situation.

He doesn't deserve to live or to have a beautiful queen like my mom. We would have the perfect family if he wasn't a part of it. All of a sudden, the sound was drowned out with music and all I could hear was Betty Wright, "Tonight is the night that you make me a woman…. I peep into the hall, to see if mom would appear and she never did.

CHAPTER THREE

I couldn't understand why daddy had to be so damn mean. I guess I'll never understand. Nothing ever seems right anymore. Years have gone by, and the feeling of emptiness has gotten worse than before. I wanted to feel needed. I was sitting on the wall of the block just thinking. The wall was made of bricks and it's where people hung out. I'm chilling in deep thoughts, and I need some type of release from reality. I'm thinking about how I wish my mama would leave my dad. My next-door neighbor was riding by, and she stopped.

"What's up?" She yelled out her car window.

"Nothing much. I replied

"You want to ride with me down to the pool hall later?" She asked me.

"Yeah, that's cool."

She told me that she would come get me later that night. I was down with it. It was exactly the escape I needed.

It's a nice hot day and it's about 96 degrees. The block is slowly beginning to get packed. OGs and wanna be's were shooting dice, which is all they seem to be interested in lately.

Guys selling dope on every corner, which seems to be all the entertainment we're gonna get around here at the moment.

Right up the road was our hood corner store called "Good Brothers". Shit, I'm about to go and steal myself something to drink and not no soda either.

Loud through the speakers of the red candy paint, custom-made Impala Chevy, that passed me on my walk to the store, I heard the radio playing YFN Lucci, "I'm just a young fly nigga.". "Now ain't this a bitch!" I thought in complete shock. It's the Bae with another chick on the passenger side. I kept walking, speeding up my pace while heading to my destination as if I didn't see him. My soul was crushed. "This nigga ain't shit!" I thought. "I knew I wasn't the only one who he was laying up with. All that talk about me being wifey material!" I realized that he was just another man failing me. In order to cope with all the things going on I had to push it all down deep, even my thoughts about everything that was happening lately. I didn't hear the guy at the cash register, but all of a sudden he got louder.

"Hurry up and buy! Hurry up and buy!"

I slowly took two MD 20/20 from the cooler and slipped them down my sweatpants. As I was leaving, I gave the store clerk my middle finger and yelled, "Fuck you!"

Sirens seemed to be coming very close to where I was standing. "I'll be damned! What does Chief Jackson want now?" I thought to myself.

"So, Nikki, what you got in your pants?" Motherfucker just had to call my government name. Sitting in the cold jail cell I could see mold everywhere and the toilet was nasty! I couldn't' wait for mama to come get me out of this filthy, hell hole! I was taken down to City Hall for shop lifting wine.

I overheard Chief Jackson tell somebody on the other end of the phone, "She will have to be in court on this one." Was he talking about me?" I thought to myself, "I'll never hear the end of this bullshit."

Yes! I was so happy to see mama's face walk through City Hall. "Let's go Nikki. Now you know better!" She stated.

"Mama, please don't tell daddy!" I pleaded all the way home with her. To my surprise she didn't tell him, and we developed an even closer bond that day.

"Oh, Nikki, by the way, your appointment will be tomorrow at 10 a.m. sharp. You need to be ready."

As we walked into the Health Department me, my other sisters, and mama were waiting.

A nurse stepped into the lobby and called my name. "Nikki?" "Yes!!!" My mom responded.

"Come with me please." The nurse said as she directed us to the back. "Please remove your clothes and put this on." It was a white cover-up gown.

"What is this?" I asked myself. While sitting on this long table and waiting for the nurse to get started, she was interrupted by a knock on the other side of the door.

"Nurse Lisa, we have an emergency in room #114. Please come and assist us." The nurse left quickly and left us unattended. We wound up having to be rescheduled for another appointment that day.

"So, girls, what do you all want to eat?" We were leaving the Health Department and we all said in unison, "KFC is what we all want mama!" and we all laughed. Eve was a heavy-set girl and she wanted most of all the food, so of course she wanted the biggest piece of chicken from the box.

"Eve, give Nikki that breast." Mama told her. My sister always knew that me and mama had a special bond that no one could or would ever understand. Things in my life started to

happen that made me more confused. All the mental abuse has overpowered my way of thinking. My grades were really slipping and were very poor. Maybe my dad was right all along. I wasn't smart enough. His way of thinking and my way of thinking were at war. Shop lifting and parties are how I dealt with many of my issues.

"Oh shit! This my jam! Here we go again!" "Pop a perk just to start up." Migo's song, Slippery, was flowing through the speakers and I was vibing to the music like no other. I'm in a zone of my own and the drinks I am taking in have clouded my vision. Bay is checking for me. Yeah, I'm swagged all the way up. Before I realize it, four guys had me surrounded me in a circle. The niggas were having their way with my young body, and I was feeling more important than ever before. I didn't even realize that I was being led to a room with a red light and no one seemed to care what was about to take place.

I woke up the next morning on the doorsteps of my apartment with my new shoes and coat gone. My mom had just bought them for me! Anxiety and depression had taken over my mind. I realized that I was dumped here with no remorse at all. "What happened? Was I raped?" I must have had a black out or something. Embarrassment was all over me. I dusted myself off and realized I couldn't handle all that alcohol; I got to do better.

The Check Up

It's only been two weeks since I fucked up with by overdoing it with the drinking. My drinking habit was out of control!

"Nikki?" Being snapped out of my thoughts.

"What's up J-dog?" J-dog was one of my little brothers.

"Please show me how to beat the next level on 'Call of Duty'." My brother said. "Oh yea! Sis, you seem to be gaining a lot of weight." His room was a mess!

"Shut up boy!" Boom! The sound of the front door slammed and as we looked up, our oldest brother was running like he had seen a ghost or something. I asked him, "What's wrong?"

"Some boys were trying to jump me!"

One thing for sure, we stood with one another. When you fucked with one, you would have to deal with us as a whole. That meant all eight of us! We all headed for the front door, and we were ready to kick some ass. People in the hood knew what it was when we pulled up. They labeled us as, a baby football team.

"Get in the house! Every last one of you!" It was Mama and we always fell under her command." What the hell y'all out here doing?" Mama asked.

We knew Mama wasn't going to punish us and she wouldn't harm a fly. "Damn, I wish she would leave daddy," I thought to myself. Later on, that week, we caught up with the boys who tried to jump my oldest brother. We took it to their ass! Every kid in our hood thought twice before trying us. Nobody wanted any beef with us for real!

Two days away from my second doctor's appointment and all type of emotions was going on inside of me and my body. I had become uneasy about a lot of things. I'm scared and confused all at the same time. 1:45 a.m. and I'm awakened with cold chills. Sweat had taken over my body. The closer it got to my doctor's appointment the more I had doubts about all of it. "What can I do to avoid this appointment?" I asked myself. Not being able to breathe and tears came rolling down. I had to take a shower that washed away my tears and let all the pain that I felt inside roll down the drain. I let it flow freely. The very first time in my life I was able to release everything that had been held deep inside of me for fourteen long years.

Wasn't I supposed to feel protected and loved instead of afraid, bitter, and uneasy? "Why me God?" I knew there had to be a God out there somewhere in this world of ours. I was thinking about how mom is always praying, and I was snapped out of my deep thought by a knock on the door of the bathroom.

"Who the hell are in there? Open this damn door, now!" my dad yelled. I jumped out the shower in a hurry and got dressed really fast without even drying off. "Take your ass to bed! What the hell you are doing up this time of night anyway?!" I rushed past him.

"Why does he have to be so mean all the time?" I thought in my mind. The person I once loved and adored, I now hated with a passion. "O fuck boy". I mumbled. I had a very long day ahead of me, so off to bed I went. I finally got some sleep after a few tosses and turns in my bed.

The sound of my alarm clock went off and I jumped out of my bed. The clock read 7:00a.m. and mama was standing in the doorway to my room, checking to see if l was up yet.

"Good morning, Nikki." "Are you okay?" she asked.

"Yes, mama. Why do you ask?"

"Just checking. Get dressed so we can leave because we have to be there by 8:00 a.m."

Today it would just be beautiful queen and me, as I call my mother. It would be so nice being able to just have her to myself,

for a change and be in her presence. While getting dressed for today I am jamming to the radio and it's playing the song by X-scape, "Work me slowly, take your time and work me slowly. Don't need a man around if he's going down too fast."
Bay had been on my mind heavily lately and I knew that he could get in so much trouble for sleeping with me. He was ten years older than me, and I plan to take that secret with me to the grave. He sure hasn't been around lately and if I was trifling, I would tell on his no-good ass, but that is just not how I rock. Besides, I did lie to him about my age, and he doesn't even know the truth about that. I couldn't understand why I wanted older guys in my life. I knew I was looking for something, but I just didn't have a clue as to what that might be. Maybe it was that father role I was looking for. I really wasn't sure and all I knew was that it didn't feel right. "Let's go!" Mama calls out.

On our way to the clinic mama tells me the reason she suggested to have me put on birth control. "It's because you are having cycles now Nikki and I don't want you having babies before you have time to enjoy life. Baby its real hard out here for young black women. Stay a child as long as you can." She told me. My beautiful queen. I love her. We pulled into the parking lot and an uneasy feeling came over me all of a sudden.

"Are you okay?" Mama could tell that I had tension in my body language.

"Yes mama. I'm good. I'm just hungry and I didn't get to grab a cereal bar before we left."

"Okay baby. We will get you something to eat after your appointment."

"Welcome back." The nurse greeted us. "We will be with you both in a second. Just have a seat." The nurse said as she pointed to the waiting area. I looked around the room hoping I didn't see anybody that I knew. Thank God, I didn't notice anybody.

"Nikki Jones?" The nurse called out from behind the desk.

"Yes?" Mama and I both answer at the same time. We followed the nurse to the
_.

back. As I was walking down the cold hallway I felt as if I was being led into a judgment room on judgment day.

"Well, Ms. Jones." The nurse stated. "I will not be able to place your daughter on any kind of birth control today. I've noticed something on her uterus, so we have to do an ultrasound to see what it can be. Nikki, you are free to get dressed now. Come to the desk up front so we can check you out before you go."

Thank you, God!" I said to myself. I had been holding my breath which seemed like forever. Mama wanted to know if I would help her cook dinner and of course I told her that I would. Another time for us to bond even closer that day.

"Mama, I love you so much and I want you to know that I appreciate you. I appreciate everything you do, and you are the best mama in the world!"

"Nikki, everybody thinks that they have the best mama in the world". She said with a smile on her face.

"Well, they are mistaken because there is nobody like you, mama and if we didn't have you, I don't know what we would do."

"You would make it because God is always right here with you, Nikki." Mama said, as she pointed to my heart. Mama had to be the smartest woman in the world.

CHAPTER FOUR

The fresh scent of lemon Pine Sol smelled so soothing throughout our home. The T.V. was tuned into CNN, world news and everybody _from the oldest to the youngest was at home cooling it. Mama has finally finished with the final touches on her fried turkey, mashed potatoes, sweet peas, and homemade biscuits. Of course, the best sweet, iced tea. Hearing that loud truck pull up once again, made everybody tense up. It is so sad that we could not even be comfortable in our own house anymore for that damn demon that was about to come in. We could already tell that all hell was about to break loose cause dad stormed in the house, without a smile or even a hello. No kiss my ass or nothing.

Boom! He slammed the bedroom door behind him leaving an echo ringing through the house. Mama kept right on setting the table and as she was preparing our plates. We already knew what the daily routine: take a bath and then go to bed after we are eating.

"Susan!" Is all we could hear coming from down the hallway in such an evil tone. Mama left the kitchen in a rush to assist my father. If she didn't, it was going to be hell to pay.

"Shut the fuck up bitch!" Slap! "Bitch I told you not to question anybody about me and my whereabouts!" The lady next door had admitted that she was having an affair with my dad, but for some odd reason, her admitting that made it seem as if mama had confronted her about it. Now mama had to pay for another mistake, that she didn't make.

The beating that dad was giving to mama seemed to last for hours. "Damn! I wish I could help her!" I yelled from my room. I really had had enough of this. Nobody deserves to be beat on and especially for something that they didn't do. My mom didn't deserve to be abused and hit like that. The next day at school I reported it to the case worker, Ms. Atkins.

"My father beats on my mom all the time, and it really gets scares me."

"I am going to make sure this is checked out, Nikki. I am sorry you are going through all this, but I will do everything that I can to make sure you and your family is protected from the abuse you all are going through." The case worker said.

"Thank you so much!" I stated with tears running down my face. 'I didn't want to tell anybody about this, but I just can't take it anymore because it hurts so bad!"

"I understand, Nikki and you did the right thing. Whatever happens now is not your fault and I need you to remember that okay?"

"Yes ma' am." I stated as I exhaled. It was as if a huge weight had been lifted off my shoulders. My family was big on privacy, and we had always been told that what happens in our house stays in our house. I had just gone against all the rules. What price would I have to pay for getting us some help? I knew that there would be one, I just didn't know what it would be. It seems as if there's always a price to be paid in the home, I live in. Good or bad, is life supposed to be like this? I knew it shouldn't be. With the report to DFACS, they followed up on it. The next day a case worker showed up at our door.

"Hello, Ms. Jones. I am Ms. Atkins, case worker from the Department of Family and Children Services. I would like to have a word with you. May I please come in?"

"Sure." Mama responded.

"Well, Ms. Jones, I'm here because of a complaint that there has been some abuse that's been taking place inside of your home." She stated. Mama's red flag went up and she refused to tell her anything. She wasn't going to risk losing her kids in no way, point blank!

"Ms. Atkin, there has been some type of misunderstanding, but everything is just fine in my home.", my mother declared. Just when everything was brought to a close, the monster I knew of as my dad came rushing through the door.

"What's going on?" Daddy asked.

"Well, hello Mr. Waxs. I'm Ms. Akin from the Department of Family and Children Services. We have reason to believe that there's some type of abuse going on here in the home." the case worker shared. Would you care to have a seat so we can discuss this matter?"

Meanwhile, I was in my room ear hustling. "Oh shit! He is gonna kill me!" I thought. Scared and shaking, I knew I had no other choice but to run.

Too Much To Handle

"Damn, I should have never run away, I think to myself." It had been two days already and I was hungry! I needed a good bath and on the days my dad wasn't at home I would stop by my house. Mama would at least find me a little something to eat.

"Nikki, your dad said you can't come home. He said to make sure all the windows and doors are locked at night, so that you won't be able to get in the house. Mama wasn't hearing any of that though. "Baby, come home." She begged as her voice cracked. I knew that no matter what the consequences were, he would have to pay it, and I couldn't afford to let that happen. Just knowing that I was safe is all that mattered to her.

"Nikki, my mom said that you can't stay here anymore, my neighbor Tasha stated to me a day later. Tasha and her mom lived four houses down from me. So, I knew I had no other choice than to go back home With that came a beating from my father without clothes on. It seemed as if every chance he got, he made sure I paid for the visit of the caseworker. My dad beat me quite often for that. Things only got worse over time. You know how people say that trouble don't last always? Well, I found that hard to believe.

Where has the time gone?! Man, I found out that time doesn't stand still for no one. We were out for summer break and my next appointment was on the agenda for today. They are doing the ultrasound and I'll be so glad when I find out what is going on with my body.

CHAPTER FIVE

"Well, congratulations Ms. Jones! You are four and half months pregnant." Really not understanding what she just said, but the tears that formed in mom's eyes as she sat next to me, were heartbreaking to my soul. I knew that she understood everything that the nurse had just said to me.

Mama looked at me and whispered, "Nikki. I can't believe it." A tear rolled down her face. The nurse told me to get dressed. "We have to start you on some vitamins as soon as possible.", She stated as she walked out to get samples. I was still in shock and couldn't believe what had just happened. How did this happen so fast? Another still moment and quietness filled the car as mama sat there and stared out the windshield for about ten minutes. I didn't say anything because I didn't know what to say. On our way home, Marvin Sapp was playing, "Never would have made it without you. I would have lost it all, but now I see how you were there for me." Mama looked over at me with a glance and the song continued. "I'm stronger; I'm wiser; I'm better, so much better." We allowed the music to invade and heal our souls. I knew that I had broken my mother's heart and it upset me. She's the queen of my life and the person I have always loved. How could I have done this? All kind of mixed feelings invaded my inner being.

Knock, knock, knock.

"Come in," I said from my bed. "Oh, hey mama." "Listen Nikki, we need to talk."
"Okay." I said.

"Listen, I don't believe in abortion, so you will have this child. Do you understand me?" "Yes, I do." I told her.
"Okay good. I'll help you raise this child. We will just keep this between us for now until I can find a way to tell your father." I grabbed mama and hugged her so tight. Her last words were, "We will get through this baby." Then she walked out.

A few days later, I told Bay about what was going on. I never really saw him again after that. "Fuck boy!" I thought. He is just like every other man. Things became too much for me to handle. My grades began to drop even more, and I skipped class as much as I could. The board of education was tired of me and my actions. I had just given up on all of it. I was put out of regular school and sent to an alternative school, where all the problem kids were. Still no effort and whatever goes was my mind set. Stealing, partying, and fighting are what I live for.

Fast Money

"Mark, what's up?" Mark was one of my partner's and he was the type of teenager that was down for whatever. 10:30 p.m. and we were chilling. Riding in Marks Camaro, all black inside and out.

We were hitting the block and I noticed that Mark had pulled up right behind an auto parts shop.

"Nikki, we are about to hit this shop up." Mark told me. "You down or what?" he asked.

"Hell yeah! I'm down with it." I was feeling like it wasn't gonna make things any worse than they already were. All black we exit the car, cutting off the alarm system and we enter our target. BINGO! We hit for $2,5000.00. We hit them up for car parts too and that was worth
$1,300.00.

"Good damn lick!" I thought. "Fast money." I said with a smile. We hit a lot more licks after that. I'm moving just like the boys and I'm chilling with them constantly. I knew that I was charring a child, but I didn't allow that to slow me down. Not at all.
"Freeze! Get on the ground and keep your hands raised above your head, where I can see them!" We had made another hit and the police had the place surrounded. We were all taken into custody.

"Damn! I done fucked up again!" I thought as I was placed in a small city jail cell. I had been down here since Saturday and here it was Wednesday. I didn't even realize how bad this looked on me or what it was doing to my family. I saw Tara and she had lost so much weight! Later I found out she had been using drugs. "What happened to you Tara?" I had to ask. "Why are you locked up?"

"I should be asking you the same thing, Nikki!" She fired back at me. I had too much on my mind, so I just brushed it shit off. I wasn't gonna entertain her, so I laid down in the cleanest spot I could find which, was in a comer. I quickly dozed off into sleep.

"Nikki Jones?" Badge #1246. Step to the front." One of the guards called out.

"Yes sir? I'm Jones."

"Let's go." He demanded.

Walking a corner of City Hall, I noticed mama standing there talking to the Chief. "What have you gotten yourself into now, Nikki?" Mama asked me. "Thanks, Chief, for calling me."
"Have a great day or try to, anyway. I'll be praying for you because I know you sure do need it." As were exiting the City Hall building, I looked at the Chief and put my middle finger up at him.
"Pray for this, fuck boy.

I said and motioned as we were walking out. I noticed that mama held a yellow piece of paper in her hand.
"What you got mama?" I asked.

"Listen, Nikki." Now she had my full attention for sure.

"What's up mama?" I said. One thing for sure, I knew mama had my best interest at heart.

"Nikki, you have got to slow your roll. You are about to have a child in a few months! Here you are, just out here wild and stuff. God knows what else. You might be going away for a while with this trouble you have gotten yourself into this time." She caught me by surprise when she said that. "Nikki, I can't get you out of this. God will see us through this though, as always and I do trust that. I can't even work a full day anymore without being called about something you have done. We have to figure out a way to address these issues, Nikki."

Push!

"Get your ass in here right NOW!" My daddy yelled.

"Here we go again with the same old shit! He's always yelling about something! I can't stand his ass!" I said to myself. "Same old shit, just another day."

"Look, you sorry little bitch, you are going to get a job around this house. I knew that you weren't gonna be shit! Your ass is out of school, out here taking people's shit. It doesn't work like that, Nikki." He went on and on with his thoughts about me. Not one good word exists in his mouth. Only if he knew he was ripping me apart, inside out. Slowly, second by second, minute by minute and hour by hour.

His words were like an open sore being filled with salt. How Dare he, when he is supposed to be my father. How can a man tear a child down the way that he does? Tears are flowing from my eyes, and I glance up only to notice the pain in my mom's eyes. I knew she wanted to hold me and tell me that everything will be alright, but she couldn't leave the spot that she was standing in. We all were at a standstill and my dad walked out the front door. He slammed it without a care in the world. Mama embraced me immediately. Like always she said, "Everything will be alright."

Push! Push! Push! "I can't do this, and it hurts so bad!" I thought and was interrupted with the voice of my mother.
"The same way it went in is the same way it's coming out, Nikki."

"Please, please, somebody help me!" I wanted to get up and walk out. I attempted to get up with that thought and mama pushed me right back down.

"Nikki, these people are going to strap your ass to this bed if you don't lay back down!" Mama informed me. Listening, I did what I was told to do. With really no strength inside me and now knowing how I was supposed to get this big thing out of me. I pushed with all that I had.

"Push! We see the head!" The doctor said. I then noticed an object that looked like a toilet plunger. Mama grabbed my hand to let me know that everything was okay, and she gave me a big smile. She told me that she still proud of me no matter what. Taking a deep breath and one more push, I had delivered a beautiful baby boy!

"Nikki, you have a boy!! 7 pounds 14 oz." Qamontae, my handsome son, was brought into this world. Being a mother so young. I still didn't understand the concept of it all and how much a responsibility this was for me. With no worries, mama took care of him, for real.

Qamontae was just like my little brother. We would get the chance to grow up with each other.

I was woken up with crying and I jumped up so fast! I knew something had to be wrong. For some reason, Qamontae, had rolled out of the bed and he had landed on the floor. Somehow, he ended up being up under my bed. "What the fuck!" I thought to myself, and I had no idea how it happened but I was so glad that he was alright and not hurt at all. I just had to have Qamontae with me, right up under me, in the bed, when I went to sleep." I have to keep a closer eye on lil man. You are a handful already."

I'm not sure if my father hated me even more now since the baby came here or not. He was so confusing, and I made it my business to stay out of his way.

"Sis, what's up?"

I didn't even notice my little brother, J-dog, standing at my room door. I had been so busy in my own little world.

"Nothing. What's up with you, bro?"

"Nothing much, but I wanted to ask you how the job search is going?" J-dog asked. "You know you have to do what you have to do, sis. I love you and I do worry about you, a lot." I hugged my little brother and told him everything is going to be just fine for us all.

"Please don't worry about nothing little brother and you just be sure to stay focused."

"Didn't I tell you the other night not to play that video game after 4:00 p.m." Daddy yelled. He caught the both of us off guard. "I'm gonna beat your ass because you don't listen to nothing, I tell your hard headed ass! YOU DON'T LISTEN!!" Raising his voice to the top of his lungs. He swung the belt, that he had been wearing, at us both. Beating both of us. It seemed like hours before he stopped. Me and my brother begged him to stop, and we promised him that we would do better. We were constantly

49

enduring a nightmare that I wished would all be a dream and when I woke up it would all come to an end. The beatings didn't stop until our father was out of breath.

CHAPTER SIX

First day at my first new job! I'm really excited and things are good. I be damn. How did me and Tara end up on second shift together? Oh, this should be fun. I was the cook at the Waffle House, and she was the waitress. "Pull one egg and drop one sausage!" Tara yelled across the floor. "An all start breakfast."

"Hold up!" I said to Tara from the grill. "Can you please slow the fuck down calling that order? You know that I'm new to this."

"Alright, alright. Just calm down King Kong." She said while laughing at me. "Pull... one sausage..." Tara was being funny now. We ended up being really good co-workers together. One of the best teams that Waffle House could ask for. One our slow days at work we had got really close and closer than most. No lie. I have always been attracted to Tar. "Damn! Tara's ass is super fat!", I thought. I decided to make move.

"So, Tara, what do you say about us chilling tonight after our shift is over?" I asked. Her dark skin was smooth as a baby's ass, head and toes. Had I become confused about my sexuality? If so, it is what it is. She just smiled at me, and I knew it was on.

"Welcome to Waffle House." Tara greeted the couple that entered. "Pork Chops plate on two, out like one." She called in that order.

We were back at Tara's spot and its 11:30 p.m. It's a Wednesday night and we are cooling. We are sipping on some

Ciroc, and Tank is singing through the speakers, "That's what you get every day when you fucking with me." It echoes throughout the small apartment of hers. I'm allowing the drinks to relax me all the way. Tara is up on the floor drinking and she's vibing to the music.

"Damn! She's a stallion." I thought to myself. Now, it's time I make my move. Up on the floor with Tara, doing my own thing, pretty much from a far. The music is flowing through the speakers. Musiq started playing, "Love, so many people use your name in vain, love, those who have faith in you sometimes go astray... " I couldn't help but to grab a hold of all the beauty that stood before my eyes. God, she's so sexy. I pull her close to me and a little closer still. We kissed instantly, right on the spot. We shared much passion in our kiss. Both of our body's couldn't help but surrender to one another's will. I kissed her slowly on the neck, then I slowly over to her ear lobes, as I reached her beautiful chest. Her nipples were brown and sexy. They stood at attention for me, wanting my lips to grab a hold of them. She begins to moan, and I was able to tell that her knees were getting weak. Tara was enjoying every moment of the pleasure her body was receiving and she then let out a small moan. I could barely hear her.

"It feels so good and right." I whisper. Tara undresses herself very slowly as I watch. I was taking every second in of her being naked. Not being able to hold myself back, I cupped one of her breasts, sucking and licking then as if it was a loose piece of candy in my mouth. My hand found its way in between her thighs. Oh, my goodness, she was so wet! Then my hand slides in naturally, in and out of her cookie jar. I'm rubbing her clit in a circle, while we are kissing none stop, we made our way to her love seat, holding one another, as if we were afraid to let go. I then placed her down gently on her back and I massaged her with my tongue all against every part of her body. Once I reached in between her thighs, I was ready to feast. Boy did I feast all night long!

The way I was eating her out, you would have thought I had missed a lot of meals.

Licking and sucking on her sweet pussy, I drank all her sweet nectar. Tara came so hard that her legs started shaking and she begged me to stop! My ring back tone with Future, my jam on it

"Wicked", woke me up! I jumped up to answer it.

"Who the fuck would be calling this time of the day?" I thought to myself. Answering the cell phone, it was my queen on the other end.

"Nikki get to this house so you can help me with this child of yours."

"I'm on the way." I said before disconnecting the call. Glad that I answered when I did, it became painfully obvious that Tara hadn't been keeping it one hundred with me. Tara hadn't told me about this young nigga she had been fucking with for almost a year. I even found out that he had been beating on her the whole time they had been dating. Not even fifteen minutes after leaving to see what's up with mama, that lame ass square busted down her door, beating her into a coma.

"Please don't hit me!" Tara begged for her life. Every time Ronnie came across her face you could hear a done breaking.

"Bitch, I warned you about how I was when we got together!" Tossing her across the floor, causing more damage.

"Please Ronnie, I'm sorry! Please stop hurting me!"

He beat her so bad causing her to become unresponsive. I was up and out of Tara's apartment within minutes after call from mama. I knew if she was calling, she must have needed me. She has always been the type of woman capable of handling whatever came in her direction and that's just the way she's always been. Last night, being with Tara, had me feeling complete. I thought to myself, "I have to keep this a secret, and no one can find out about this." That thought played over and over in my head. "My dad would really think I'm a piece of trash if he knew about it." Sometimes I often wonder, "Am I even worthy to be labeled as a human being? All I ever wanted was a normal life."

CHAPTER SEVEN

"Stop it right where you are!" I heard a deep steel voice coming from behind me.

"What the fuck is going?" I stopped right in my tracks, following my last instruction. Looking

over my shoulder, there were two cops, that had two nines pulled out, pointed in my direction. "What's up now?" I asked the two pigs.

"You know what's up, Nikki."

"I ain't did nothing." I said back to them. "Besides, I'm headed home, minding my own business. I just jumped off the bus, so what is it y'all want with me?" They weren't listening to nothing I was saying. No matter, what they have always labeled me as a problem. I was thrown into the back of the cold leather seat of the police are. The handcuffs were so tight around my wrist it caused me to be in a lot of pain. J-dog was inside of the comer store, watching what was taking place on the outside, from a far. The police had stopped me right in front of the hood comer store, "Good brother".

"Nikki!" My little brother called out. It really hurt for my brother to have to witness me getting arrested. He came running out the store almost trippin over his untied air forces. "Nikki!" He called out. "What's going on sis?"

"I don't know bro, but I need for you to go home and let mama know what's going." "OK." He took off running fast as hell, like his life depended on his destination.

"Damn! Here we go again." I thought to myself, while standing in front of the chief once again. It wasn't anything new to me. His big, pop belly ass. "He needs to Jose some weight, fat motherfucker." I was thinking before I was interrupted out of my thoughts.

"Well, well, well, Ms. Jones. You didn't show up for court. There's a warrant here on my desk for you."

"Get real!" I told him, in a very loud voice, filled with rage and anger.

"I see some things in life don't ever change." His smart ass said. "By the way, it's real." I dropped my head because there was nothing I could say. I was being transported to a detention center, all the way up state, until another court date was set. I felt lost, hurt, and mad. No matter how hard I try to walk in the right direction, shit still doesn't up right. The hell with everything. I'm about to enter into a while different world of its own.

"Gate 26! On the west-side wing!" One of the correctional officers called over his radio. While listening to what's about to take place, the sound of the huge steel gate, with razor wire wrapped all around it, from the button to the top, opening and it sent chills all the way up my spine. Mama came to visitation every week and so did my precious baby boy. My father never showed his face, and I was so glad because I could hear his ass now, "She ain't shit! She will never be shit!" I was so happy he didn't come to visit. Anyway, I was tired of being broken in spirit. Hell, I get it, I ain't shit. My court date had finally arrived. The courtroom was packed with a bunch of families.

"Calling case number 1520106 docket file #1200, Jones." I wasn't really listening to me being called. "Do we have a Jones in the courtroom today?" Judge Williams asked.

"Yes sir." My attorney spoke up.

"Please, step forward with your client." He instructed him. He approached the bench and I listened to the judge and my attorney discuss me right in front of my face, like I wasn't there. I was slackened by what the judge said.

"90 days in boot camp, Ms. Jones,"

"WHAT!" I couldn't believe what he said to me. "Boot camp! What the hell is that supposed to mean?"

"Ms. Jones?" The judge said, facing me as if I was wrong.

"You have one more time, to have one of your disrespectful outbursts, inside of my courtroom and I'm going to send you down the road for 180 days." Down the road I went. Sent for 90 long days of my life. It seemed as if minutes were hours, hours seemed as if they were days and days seemed as if it had been long months. I had been stripped from everything. While sitting in the back of the patrol car being transferred to the boot camp facility. I thought to myself. "If it ain't one thing it's another."

From that moment on I chose to live life just for the present moment that I was in. Being away from my family was really hard. At one point, I didn't feel I could make it. "I don't have the best family in the world, but that are my family and I love them." I was thinking, before crying myself to sleep many of those nights.

"Fifteen minutes is all you have in that shower offender." Officer James said from her desk, where she sat to monitor the entire dorm.

"Yes ma'am." I never thought that I would be in a situation such as this. That day was the very first day of my mental breakdown. I was back in my cell, balled up in the corner, rocking back and forth. Shaking uncontrollably.

"Offender Jones, are you okay?" I didn't say a word. I just kept rocking back and forth. Back and forth I was shaking all over. The officer noticed that she wasn't getting a response, so she called for backup on her radio. "Any available units, I need assistance on A and K range." Before I knew it, I was placed in a room, inside a paper gown, without no sheets, and the room was freezing! It was so nasty, with paper all over the place. Surely death had to be better than this. "God if you are real, please let me die. I can't take life anymore and it's too hard to bear." Nothing happened and the pain was still there.

CHAPTER EIGHT

"Help! Somebody 911!" Mama was yelling and crying, rushing to see what was going on with Qamontae. He was not breathing! Mama was in tears and 911 responded to the call pretty fast. My baby was being rushed to the emergency room. The doctor was able to get him into stable condition. Later on, we found out that he only had one good lung. The cause of his condition was from being born early. Mama waiting on Qamontae hand and foot until he was well again, and she was not having it any other way. She protected him as if her life depended on it.

It's 10:30 a.m. A rainy, cozy day. Momma was out doing her regular shopping. Knowing that we were not allowed to enter mama's bedroom, I had to be the hardheaded one. I went in mama's room to watch her 64-inch T.V. There was a show box that seem to be out of place to me. My curiosity got the better of me and I wanted to know what was in the shoe box. I climbed off the bed and reached for the box.

"What are you doing in here?" My brother, Hitta, asked me.

"SHUT UP!" I fired back at him. "I do what I want to do!" While giving him the business I opened the box. Instead sat a nice 25.

"WHOA! PUT THAT DOWN!" Hitta demanded me. I was holding it and pointing it in his direction. All of a sudden, the gun went off.

"Amazing grace, how sweet the sound, that saved a wrench life me, I was once was lost, but now I'm found, was blind but now I see." The choir sung from behind the pull pit. Many people were moved by the spirit as mama would say. Pastor Walker approached the pull pit and greeted the congregation.

"We will be reading from Proverbs 3:5&6, the NIV version. Trust in the Lord GOD with all of your heart. Lean not to your own understanding and in all of your ways acknowledge Him and he will direct your path." Weeping and crying is all you could hear.

"GOD, I surrender as mama cried and held her hands up in the air. As church was being let out, mama walked up to Pastor Walker and asked for prayer. "Pastor Walker, can you pray with? My family seems to always be in an uproar and there seems to never be any peace."

"Yes, Ms. Jones. When two or more are together God is always in the mist." After being prayed for Pastor Walker, suggested that mama bring her family to church the following Sunday.

A still voice spoke to her and said, "Raise a child up in the way he or she should go, and they will never depart from it." She wondered was that God speaking? After a very long day, we were all tired. Mama was just trying to get a hold of things in her life. "What lays ahead for me?" She asked herself. Mama began to think back to when she was young girl. "Growing up, I had a really good childhood." Mama thought. "In school, I was one of the top ten in my class. Has my life been cursed?" Mama seemed to just brush her thoughts away.

Pulling into the driveway, mama noticed a police car was there. "What now! My kids are always into something is all I can say." Mama jumped out of the car in a hurry, and she already had a headache. "What's going?" Mama asked the officer.

"Well Ms. Jones, I caught these two young men stealing off a beer truck. Right in front of the Texaco store in the middle of town. "Now, I will not report it this time, but the next time, I will. Consider this a slap on the wrist." Mentally tired of these boys after walking off.

"Oh, and by the way officer, thank you very much." Mama said to the officer as she was walking toward the house. "I just don't have the strength for this anymore. I lost my job and I'm collecting social security from David's check. That's not enough to live on, DAMN IT!"

"Mama, mama. I'm hungry." Gain said.

"Okay baby, let me figure something out. Shit, I'll have to get twelve pack of noodles and a pack of ground beef. That is what's for dinner tonight. It's called making something out of nothing." Everyone ate and we all went to bed full. I:45 a.m. and I heard a whisper. "Heaven, somebody is looking in our window."

"Who's out there?" Heaven yelled. Whoever it was took off running in the woods Another day in the life of many struggles. Mama is up and ready for her food stamp appointment. The struggle has become real! While getting dressed inside of her bedroom, she noticed that a picture frame was out of place. She picked the picture frame up, to move it back to its original place and she noticed a bullet hole in the wall.

"What the fuck?" Mama said. "Nikki!" My name was the first name she called out. "Nikki, get your ass in here!"

"What's up?' I asked.

"What is this!" Mama asked, while pointing at the wall. "What's what?" Nikki said, acting dumb.

"You know damn well what I'm talking about!" That was the first time I ever really heard mama raise her voice. She has always been the humble type.

"Okay mam. I will admit, I was playing with your pink gun, and it went off." She didn't know it was only an inch away from Hitta's head.

"Don't be in my room when I'm not here! Do you hear me talking to you lil girl!" Mama had jacked me up lightly. "Now get out of here and close my door behind you." That day, mama had so many different feelings, that words couldn't explain. While driving to the Department of Family and Children Service, mama called her sister Annette. Annette picked up.

"Hello, what's wrong?" She asked.

"A lot! I just need someone to talk to about my kids. My kids are wild and out of control. Nikki is always into something I just don't what I'm going to do with her. If something happens to any of my kids, I don't know what I would do with myself. I'll never be able to forgive myself. I have to get rid of that gun."

"You just do what you feel is right, Susan. "Her sister told her. "I know that we haven't really been that close since middle school. But I want you to know, I feel that you have always made good choices in your life."

"Annette, I do feel that sometimes I need that fun for my own protection. Did you know that I let David back into my life again? That man thinks I belong to him and only him." Mama said. "He has made it known." It was time to end her long conversation with her baby sister. She looked up and she had reached her destination. Before hanging up, mama told her sister that she loved her and they promised to see one another soon, but will that promise come to pass?

Strong Black Woman

"Stop running in my house, like y'all have lost your mind or something! I'm trying to clean up. Now, get outside, in that front yard until I'm done.

"Mama, John wants to know if it would be alright, if he came by later today?" Eve asked.

"I guess so. Hell, the two of you have been seeing each other for a while now, anyway.

Mama said, "Nikki, come and ride with me to the store to drab some meat for the grill, today. By the way, tell J-dog and Knot I said to pull the pool out and fill it up with water." Mama was in an awesome mood today. It's very nice outside and it's the middle of June, about 85 degrees. After we got back from the store, the family began to entertain one another, and mama got down on the grill. We ate leg quarters, pork ribs pork chops, potato salad, and baked beans with brown sugar, pretty much a good soul good meal on the grill. R. Kelly was singing, "Step, step, side to side, now let me see you do the love slide." It was the type of day we all remember.

Daddy was no fun at all. He sat under the oak tree, really not talking to anybody. It seemed as if he had been in his own little world. He was the type of father that was hard to understand or figure out. Daddy left shortly after mama fixed him a plate of her delicious food. After a long happy day with the family, it was about time to wind it down. The little crowd started to thin out. Everyone teamed up and helped clean.

"Give it to me now! Mama!", Gain shouted from the top his lungs.
"What do you want child?" Mama asked Gain.

"J-dog and Knot won't give me MY BIKE!" Gain yelled. WHOOP WHOOP!

"There they go again with all that fighting." Mama said. "Stop!" Mama told them. "Go inside and get a bath." They did what she told them to do.
"Mama, can I sleep with you?" Nikki asked mama. It was 9:30 p.m.

"Yes, come on in baby. You sure can sleep with me." I lay down next to her. Then I asked her to tell me a little about her life when she was a young girl. Of course, she did. To me mama had always been a strong black woman no matter what. She went through a lot in her life, but she still seemed to embrace the situation. "Well, I did finish school and once I finished, then I got married. I left home to live with my husband's family."

"So, were you married before you met my father?" Nikki asked her.

"Yes baby. I was married before I met your father. I think that I need to explain it to you a little, so that you'll understand where I'm coming from. Your oldest sister and brother have the same father. You and your youngest brothers have the same father." Mama explained.

Now, I understand." I told her.

"Let me finish telling you young lady. You wanted to hear this, so don't interrupt." Mama pulled me even closer to her in a bear, like hug. I loved being next to her. There's nothing like a mother loved. Something about it allows a child to feel safe.

"I love this woman." I thought.

"Mason, who was my husband before I met your dad, was killed inside of a pool hall. He used to gamble back in the old days, and they say that he was the man in the streets back then."

Mama got a far-a-way look in her eyes and I knew she was remembering better days.

KNOCK! KNOCK! A loud noise was coming from the living room. "Somebody gets the DAMN DOOR!" I opened the front door what I saw caught me by surprise!

"What is he doing back here?" Daddy had his luggage in his left hand smiling from ear to ear. "Now, I know he's not moving back in." Nikki said, while walking away from the door. Just when our family was starting to be halfway normal, here he comes Satan himself.

"Get back here, you little nasty bitch!" Afraid of what would come next, I followed his command. "GRAB THESE BAGS and yes I'm moving back in. Since I've been gone, y'all have gotten out of control! I run this shit!" He was sure to remind me. With that being said he walked in, shoulders back and head held high, as if he was a king of this castle.

"How much is it going to cost to rent a U-Haul so, we can get your things moved out of here, Eve?" Now that's sad that mama has let daddy talk her into putting her oldest daughter out.

"I'm going to miss you sis!" I said, while crying my eyes out. "Why do you have to move?" I asked. I pleased with my oldest sister not to go with big tears falling from face.

"Come here." Eve grabbed Nikki and held her, trying to console Nikki the best way she could. It seemed to take Eve and hour just to get her to calm down a little. "Listen." She was saying, while holding the bottom of Nikki's chin, lifting her head to be able to make eye contact with her baby sister. "Nikki, you will always be my little sister. We have a bond that no one can break. Do you understand me?" Eve asked Nikki. "You are always welcome to come spend the night with me, okay?"

BUMP! BUMP! "YO GET IT, GET IT, THAT'S THE WAY, YOU GONE GIRLS!!"

Man, this house party is popping! Eve's house party was live as fuck! Everybody in the joint that night got wasted. I woke up the next day with a major headache! Being at my sister's house, I was able to do whatever I chose to. "My house had become too controlling since mama let daddy back in her life." Nikki said to her sister. "Now, how did this happen!" I woke up the next day, after the party. Still at my sister's house and guess who was lying beside me? Tara! Naked as a jay bird! I was so confused! My sister walked in and was shook at what she saw.

"I KNEW YOU LIKED GIRLS!" Eve said to Nikki.

"Will you please close the door?" I asked her. I chose not to see Tara anymore after that day. Anyway, I was back in my old neighborhood.

"What's up! Long time no see, Nikki!" The boys on the block dapped me up. "Where have you been for these last few months, homie?"

"I been with my oldest sister, at her new spot, cooling. My auntie only lived a few houses down where the block was. Just chilling on the comer, in the hood, were the best days. While chilling, I noticed that there was a big commotion going on in my aunties back yard. It was my daddy's sister. "WHAT'S GOIN ON?!" I asked one of my childhood friends.

"What the fuck?! That's your dad, Nikki! It looks like he's about to fight or cut somebody up!" One of my friends said. We all moved in that direction to see what was going on. I fell back behind the crowd; do I wouldn't be noticed. As I got a little closer, I saw that Qamontae, is sitting on the passenger side of daddy's truck. Qamontae was crying his little eyes out and the door to his truck is standing wide open.

"What the hell." I mumbled to myself. "This crazy bastard, has my child out here, in theses streets, while he's about to fight?" Running in the direction of the truck I grabbed my son and ran as fast as I could. "Hey Eve, some pick me up." I told her over my cellphone.

"What's going on." She asked. I told her what was going on and she was there in fifteen minutes, after we disconnected. I wasn't having that type of thing going on around my son, if I could help it. I'm back at my sister's house. I was thinking I would just have to deal with the consequences later. I dialed up mama and I told her what just happened. She wasn't happy about it at all.

It's 11:00 p.m. and I just be damn! "Susan, not don't you know that Nikki's fast ass came and took that child out of my truck?!" Mama acted as if she wasn't sure what was going on. "I tell you one thing, she better not bring him back, since she wants to take him out of my truck.

Let's see if she can handle raising him." Daddy told mama, before he walked out.

Being at Eve's house, I pretty much had moved in with her. Having Qamontae along, slowed things down a lot in my life. Things had become more of a challenge for me, and I really didn't know one thing on how to raise a child. "Please." I pleaded with mama over the phone. "Can I just bring him back to you?" I asked.

"I don't know. Let me see if I can convince your dad. Mama said, "You shouldn't have taken him from the truck in the first place. Your dad isn't going to let anything happen to Qamontae."

"Momma, I didn't trust the movement." I told her before hanging up. "Boy, I tell you the truth, momma I such a humble person."

CHAPTER NINE

There was a really light whisper. "Shhhhh, don't say nothing." It woke me up. It was my brother-in-law, trying to take my pants off.

"NO! Get your hand off of me I told him. Now, you know this isn't right, so get off of me. NOW!" I told him twice.

"I'll pay you." He said. "Just let me taste it, Nikki, damn!

"Now, I'm going to ask you one more time to get off of me." I told him. Somehow, I was able to get loose and I rushed out of the room in a hurry. All along that nasty dog has been looking at me. "I really can't tell my sister." I thought. I knew it would tear her apart because she loved this man. I plan to just stay my distance. I'll figure something out soon, but I just don't understand why men have to cheat when they have a good woman at home. I don't know who my brother-in-law thinks he is, but his best bet is to stay away from me.

I do remember the old people use today, "A dick doesn't have a conscious and a pussy doesn't have a face." For some reason or another, he kept trying to have sex with me. Somehow, I talked mama into letting me and Qamontae come back to stay with her. I had only one option and that was to get a job. "Here we go again." I thought to myself. One thing for sure, I had to do what I had to do. Living with my sister wasn't going to work. The situation with my brother-in- law was getting out of hand. "Welcome to Zaxbys. How may I help up?" I asked, while speaking into the microphone at the drive thru. "That will be $11.50. Please drive around to pick up your order."

YES! I'm at it again. On the clock, nine to five! One thing is for sure, I have always been able to catch a job. BUZZ! BUZZ! The vibration of my phone goes off. "Now, who could be calling me this time of day?" Looking down to see who it could be, it was Tara calling. I couldn't answer, because my workplace was busy from the exit door to the counter. I could not afford to lose my job. I'll never live to tell a soul about it by the time my father got a hold of me.

"Now David, why are you leaving out this time of night? It's 1:30 in the morning." Mama asked daddy.

"BITCH! Don't you dare ask me that question again!" He fired back. "I do what the hell I want to!" He reminded her. "Now, take your ass back to bed!" he demanded mama.

"Can you please stay home tonight? Ever since you been back home, you seem to have more and more late-night business to handle." Before she knew it, David reached and grabbed a tight hold of mama. She then took off running, trying to escape. She slipped and hit her head.

BOOM! Is all you could hear throughout the silent house. She cried out from the pain, "No please, don't hit me, David." Daddy didn't care that she was pleading. Nikki was standing in the hallway witnessing the whole thing.

STOMP! STOMP! The sound of David's boots was making contact with mama's head. I closed the bedroom door and climbed out my bedroom window running as fast as I could for help! The people that live next door called the police for me.

"Thank you!" Nikki said. The first person on the scene was my uncle. He had worked for the police force for many years. He had a few words with my father and then asked daddy to leave for the night.

"That's what he wanted all along. Dirty bastard!" I thought. That night, my father got a slap on the wrist, for what happened. My father is still pissed, and he knows that I called the law on him. As he is pulling out of the driveway, Eve pulls up. She doesn't seem to be happy about what just happened. "Only if I could kill his ass", Nikki though. I dismissed the thought and went back to bed where I had been in the first place. Maybe it would be a better day tomorrow.

TAP, TAP, TAP... A real light noise was coming from the front of the house. I headed in that direction to see what was going on. It was somebody at the door. Opening the door, I was surprised to see my father standing there! It fucked me all the way up! He had such an aggressive look in his eyes and dear took over my body immediately. I took off running for safety.

Somehow, I tripped laying in the middle of the hallway of our home. There he was, standing over me, with one leg up, about to stomp me! Something inside of him caused him to just turn around and walk away. It had to be God. Feeling so close to death.

Hate, rage, scared, depression, and suicide began to invade my mind. Reaching the point in life, where I was just tired of living in such an unhealthy environment. It seemed, as if every second, I had to relive a nightmare that wouldn't go away. I was remembering every struggle and not once being able to move on from it. "I don't want to feel!" I told God. Hell, the law seems to be in favor of daddy, so it's like a no win, situation. There seem to be no help.

"Somebody! Somebody, please call 911!" The police pulled up, but David was nowhere to be found. The police finally caught up with daddy and mama found out he was being detained, down at the city jail. They arrested him early one morning around 3:30 a.m. A bond was set after a week of David sitting in jail. The county court set a date for a later time.

Walk By Faith

"OMG! GO!" NO, NO! Can somebody please bring me a knife or something sharp?!" J- dog came into the room running. "Nikki, Nikki, can you hear me honey? Don't you give up, hang in their baby! Mama's here!" Hanging from her bedroom ceiling, Nikki was clinging to her life. Time, as it was, was slipping through our hands. I wasn't able to breathe, and I felt someone at the bottom of the chair lifting me up. My air supply was being cut off slowly from my body.

"Hurry up and die!" I thought to myself. I was going in and out of consciousness and I could hear the voice of my loved ones around me. The sweet sound of mama's voice is what kept me the entire time, I believe,

"Hang in their baby," Mama told me. Finally, mama was able to cut some of the rope and I was set free from a slow death. Now, I understand when people claim to see the light while facing death, because that day I saw the light. That's something I will never forget. That's the very first time I really tried to commit suicide; mama made sure to spend a lot more time with me. She really didn't allow me to be out of her sight for too long. There's nothing like a mother's love.

A few months had passed. "God, I've made up my mind to give everything to you." Mama said. Sitting there in her dark bedroom, which seemed to be many hours, mama just prayed and cried. Just asking her higher power for mercy that day. "Lord, my life has been up and down for so many years. Being abused, which seems to be on a daily basis. My kids have gotten out of control and Nikki wants to take her own life. I just can't take it anymore, Lord. I surrender it all to you today." Mama was in a very deep conversation with God, and you would have thought that He was in her room, literally. One thing for sure, she had a really close relationship with the Guy above.

The next day, we all were headed in the direction of a church. That didn't mean that everything was good and there were still moments when we would still hear cries from behind the door of our parents' bedroom. The more momma drew to the Lord and church; the better things became for her.

"I now baptized you in the name of the Father, The Son, and the Holy Ghost!" Pastor Walker said, before dipping all eight of us in the river. Pastor Walker kept talking, "Walk by faith and not by sight." Is what he preached on that day. All of us kids had been baptized that day. Our spirit had been made new, but our human body remained the same. We all walked out of the church and mama felt like a brand-new woman, on the inside.

It's another long, hot day of summer! "Mama, what's on the menu today?"

"Well, I think I'll make some good, old, homemade, coleslaw with some hot dogs and chips today. Something light for you guys.
"Who the fuck moved my beers!" David yelled from the top of his lungs.

Well, there's nothing new about that. We tried not to pay him any attention because things could get a lot worse if we fed into it. So, everybody stayed as far away as they could.

"Now you listen, David." Momma told him. "I'm tired of this abuse and I want you out today!"
"I tell you what, Susan. I'll find me somewhere else to go!" Daddy said.

"I tell you what, asshole! You can do whatever you want to." Mama said as she walked out and never looked back. The only thing she left with was a few clothes and maybe a half of bag of supplies. Not being sure if she had made the correct choice or not, she was wondering if she made a big mistake. "Will this be the biggest mistake that I've ever made?" she asked herself. What will be the price that must be paid for the door unknown that lays ahead.

CHAPTER TEN

It's 1:00 p.m. in the afternoon, sic months later. "Okay, I see she thinks she's smart. I know her every move, so thinking she can just tell me that she's moving on and I'll be fine with it? Hell naw! It doesn't work like that Susan, and you know it!" David said to his self, while sitting in his car, watching Susan from afar. "It will be over my dead body, before I let anybody

have her!" He said. David was in his feelings so deep that he couldn't even thing straight. With all type of emotions going on, while sitting there watching Susan, listening to K-Ci sing, "If you think you're lonely now wait until tonight girl", David thought he was gonna lose his mind! HE decided to give Susan's cell phone a ring, just to see if she would pick up for him.

"Hello, this is Susan. Please leave a message" Susan's voicemail came on.

"Damn it! I know that bitch see it's me calling!" David said, before hitting the dashboard of his truck.

"David!" Lee said, snapping him out of his deep thought. "David, you have to let that woman go and live your life." Deep down in his soul, David could. He had loved this woman for twenty years!

It's not that simple, Lee! I can't just let her go and she belongs to me!" David said.

"Mama!" J-dog came running in the house, from a long day of school. "Mama, it looks like daddy's truck is parked on the next street! I think he is watching our house."

"Calm down baby. I'll handle everything, don't worry. We will get past this, J-dog. Now, go and do your homework." A few weeks had passed, and David's behavior was beginning to get out of control.

"Why do I have to live in fear?' Mama thought. "Lord, have mercy on me!" She sent a silent prayer up above. "I really feel as if I need to take a temporary protective order out on his ass." She thought to herself. It's 3:30 in the morning and my alarm is going off. "Nikki! Nikki!" Mama yelled.

"Yes mama." I answered. "Is everything okay?" Mama asked.

"No, I think somebody just tried to break in the back door. Call 911!" I yelled.

"How may I help you?" The operator asked.

"Can you please send someone out to this address? I think somebody just tried to break into my house." Mama said.

"Yes ma'am. I'm sending someone out to help you right now."

"Thank you so much!" mama said and hung up the phone. "They are on the way y'all."

"Thank God!" Nikki said. Sitting in the woods, watching the police from a far, was David's crazy ass.

"DAMN! I ALMOST GOT CAUGHT!" David said out loud to himself. "Susan will pray for this shit. Got me out here, running around, checking for her and shit."

"Mama!" Nikki called. "I have something important to tell you." "What's up?" Mama asked Nikki.

"Well, the streets have been talkin."

"What do you mean by that, Nikki?" Mama asked.

"Well, I asked one of my folks to put their ear to the ground and let me know what's being said. While I was in the hood the other day, one of the trap boys said that they have been served daddy dope." Nikki was telling Susan.

"What?" Mama asked.

"Yeah! He's smoking that shit! That's just part of what I heard. Nigga's are saying that he also said that he's going to kill you, mama! You and the dude you are dating. What are we gonna do, mama? You know he is crazy, so please be careful!" Nikki told her mama."

"Everything is going to be alright baby, so stop all that worrying. Besides, you can't always believe everything you hear in those streets, Nikki, and you know that." Mama was saying, while she was answering the front door. "Oh, hey Tara. Nikki, its Tara.

"J-dog, can you tell Tara I'll be out in a second." For some reason or another I felt like she was on some bullshit. "Tara, what's up?' She was mad as hell!

"So, all I want to know is, why haven't you been calling me? I know your ass has been avoiding my calls! You must have thought that me letting you eat my pussy was a game, huh?

That's what you thought Nikki? Oh, you had time for me when you had your mouth all over me though, right?" Tara asked.

"I really haven't had the time to call you, Tara." I told her. SLAP, SLAP, SLAP! Before you knew it, she hit me upside my face, causing my head to slam against the hard wooden door.

"Why the fuck are you putting your hands on me? You done loss your damn mind, Bitch! I screamed at Tara.

"I know game when I hear it motherfucker!" Don't fucking play me! How you gonna do this shit to me?!" I was holding Tara's hands while she was carrying on like a child, to keep her from hitting me. I know what she was saying, but I just didn't have time for this type of shit in my life right now. Hell, I didn't know if I was confused about my sexuality or what. I just had too much going on as it was. People trying to break into my house and my daddy out there talking crazy. Anything could pop off right now!

"Look at you! This the type of shit I don't need right now, Tara! I got too much going on as it is and I don't need any more drama in my life, at this point. We may have made this work, IF you would have talked to me like a grown woman and listen to the shit I got going on. You don't care though, because you too busy acting like a child! Now, get the fuck on before I hurt you, for real girl! Nobody touches my face, bitch!" With that I pushed her ass back and she walked out with tears in her eyes. That was the last time I would see her.

If I Can't Have Her, No One Can

"It's the weekend, baby!" I was telling one of my co-workers. Months had passed and mama had not heard anything from daddy, but you know what they say, there's always the quiet before the storm.

"So, Nikki. I think it's time to start allowing Thomas to come by the house. Besides, it's been a while since me and your daddy has seen each other. What do you think?" Mama asked me.

"Whatever makes you happy, mama. I'm down for it. He treats you good and I get a good vibe from him. You deserve to be happy. She smiled and with that being said, mama decided to move forward with her life. Thomas began coming by the house, getting to know the rest of the family. Things seem to be going good for everyone and we were all getting close to Thomas. He kept a smile on Mama's face, which is beautiful, just like her. While Thomas was out shopping, something caught him by surprise. David pushed up on him with his finger pointed in Thomas's direction.

"You listen to me, and I want you to listen to me good. "David told Thomas. " This is my first warning and it's my last, I want you to stay the hell away from my family, motherfucker!"

David told him, before walking away like nothing never happened.

"Come on Nikki. If you're going to the mall, I don't have all day." Eve said. Jumping in my sister's ride, I thought about it being mama's first night out, on a date and it's about time.

Shit, it's been a long time since she's been out. I was headed to Macy's to find mama a nice outfit.

"It's the middle of fall and the weather is still nice. A nice sundress should do the trick. I thought. I wanted momma to be SUPER CUTE. I had been saving money since the very first check from Zaxby's.

"LOOK! This dress is nice, Eve. What do you think? You think she will like it?" I asked Eve.

"No! It looks like you would bury somebody in that dress, Nikki." Eve said.

"I think that it's nice, so I'm going to get it for her. I ain't studying you." I said. I bought it and we went home.

"Hey! What y'all doing?" Mama asked, as she walked through the front door. "Go and get those bags out the car for me." J-dog and Knot did what they were told to do. After getting settled in from a long day, mama just wanted some peace. Nikki was sitting and watching the Maury show. Mama joined her. "So Nikki, what's been going on with you?" Mama asked Nikki. "We really haven't been able to talk much lately."

"Nothing much lately. Just been cooling and trying to lay low, staying out of trouble,

"Well baby, that's always good to hear. I need for you to always stay focused. I am very proud of you, and I love you." Mama said.

"Okay mama. I will. Thank you for saying that cause I really needed to hear that."

"Nikki, guess what I dreamed last night, girl? I dreamed that Heaven was being chased by some man!" Mama said.
"What did you do?" Nikki asked.

"Are you going to let me finish telling you or what, Nikki?" Susan and Nikki shared a really close bond.

"My bad. Go ahead." Nikki said.

"Anyways, I couldn't see the man's face, so I don't know who he is. Nikki the dream seemed so real to me that when I woke up, I was soak and wet with sweat. What really scared me was that he killed her."
"Mama, it was only a dream." Nikki said.

"I know, but it still freaked me, girl." They both smiled and cuddled, while they finished watching the show.

CHAPTER ELEVEN

Its late in the afternoon and the sun is about to go down. That's the best time to hang on the block. While I was walking, on my way to the bootleg to grab me a cold one, I heard a deep voice behind me, call out my name. "Shit, I'm always on point in the streets and my mama ain't raise no stupid bitch." Nikki thought. I looked back to see what's up. It was my daddy! "Shit, what could he possibly want", I thought to myself, as I got my shit together real fast. He pulled up on me.

"Hey Nikki, can I talk to for a minute?" David asked.

"Sure, what's up pops?" I asked.

"Listen, there's a few things I have been thinking about and I need to tell you

something." He said.

"Okay, go ahead and tell me." I really didn't know how to take him. Hell, he has always been so rude and mean. He was being nice for a change, so I was curious to see what he had on his mind.

"I just want y'all to know that I love y'all and I know I have been really hard on y'all. I am sorry about taking y'all for granted.

People don't know a good thing until it's gone." My daddy confessed to me.

Oh, my God! I think I saw a tear slide from his eyes or am I trippin? I thought to myself. "Listen, I just want my kids to be better than me and not like me." David said.

"I understand." I said, before we departed from each other. Hell, I didn't know what to say it all caught me by surprise I really needed a drink! I couldn't get to the bootleg fast enough.

It's now 1:30 a.m., early Saturday morning. J-dog has the house to his self. He met a girl named Snowflake a few weeks ago, so she was there with him.

"Do you hear something, J?" Snowflake asked.

"Naw, I didn't hear anything. I think you might be trippin." J-dog told her. He wanted to be sure she wasn't trippin, so he checked to see if everything' was good.

"What the fuck?" J-dog said, in a low tone, when he got to the back door. He noticed that it was somebody on the other side of the door, trying to pry the door open, so he could get in.

Grabbing the iron bat that sat behind the door, J-dog was prepared to knock a nigga out! When he pulled the door open, what he seen had him shook! "What's going on pops?" J-dog asked David. David was standing there with an evil look on his face.

"Where is your mama?" David asked.

"I don't know daddy." J-dog told him. David left when-dog told him that. "Nikki, Nikki!" J

"What's up J-dog? You alright? What's wrong, calm down." Nikki said. "No, I'm not alright!"
"What's going on?" Nikki asked.

"David's been here looking for mama while you were gone to the store." J-dog told Nikki. "I caught him though, trying to break in!"
"What!" Nikki exclaimed.

"Yeah, and he had this evil ass look on his face, man." J-dog told his ster. Nikki could tell it had her brother shook.
"What did you tell him?" Nikki asked.

"I told him she wasn't here and that I didn't know where she it, that's it." J-dog was all shaken up. Fear and uncertainty were all in the atmosphere. I had my partner with me.

"Mark, we have to go and find mama. We got to make sure she's safe!"
"You ain't said nothing but a word. Let's ride." Mark told Nikki, as they were walking out the door. All of our friends loved Susan too and they knew a lot about what was going on, so they understood the seriousness of the situation. It's 2:15 a.m. and we have tom the city down looking for mama. The only place left to check was Thomas' spot. His house sat far back off the road and it was surrounded with nothing but trees. "How can somebody stay all the way back here?" Mark asked. "I like the city, and this

reminds me why I wouldn't live in the country. Shit, I guess I am just too nosey." Mark said, while he was laughing.

"Hell, I don't know." Nikki said to him. "You right though, you sure are nosey motherfucker. Listen, on the real, I'm here on one mission and that's to get my mama home safe." Nikki told her friend. They jumped out the car once it was in park. Nikki knocked on the door for a minute. "Damn, is anybody here?" Nikki was getting frustrated because she was so worried about her mama. Finally, somebody from the other side of the door answered.

"Who is it?" A voice from the other side of the door called out.

"Yo! Is my mama here, Thomas? This Nikki." Nikki stated. Thomas opened the door. "Yeah, hold on a minute." Thomas said. "Is everything okay?"

"Yeah, I'm just looking for my mom. Thomas left the door hallway open, while calling Susan and letting her know that Nikki was here and wanted to see her.

"I'll be out in a minute." Susan said. "Let me get dressed." Her voice echoed throughout the house.

"Please hurry!" Nikki yelled back. Fifteen minutes later, David came out the bushes where he had been hiding. He had a long knife in his hand.

"Oh my God! Close the front door!" Nikki yelled, as she was walking away. She was hoping that they could hear her. Thomas closed and locked the door just in time, before David was able to enter. Nikki and Mark both jumped back inside of the car. They locked all doors in hopes that they would be safe. The look

David had in his eyes, was pure evil. We had never seen him in such a rage as this before. Nikki told Mark, "We got to get help!" "I know, but we don't have a phone, so what are we gonna do?!" Mark asked. David was trying to kick the door in.

"Do you want me to try and keep your mama safe while you drive and get some help, Nikki? Mark asked. Without many choices, we had to make a move and we didn't have much time. Nikki jumped behind the wheel and Mark is now out of the car grabbing an iron chair cause it's the only weapon that he could use. Nikki drove out of Thomas' driveway with the peddle to the floorboard. Nikki had Mark's car wide open on the highway as she went to get help. Finally making it to the nearest police station, she jumped out and rushed in to get assistance.

"Please! Please! I need help! My mama needs help! My father just came out of the woods with a knife!", I screamed with urgency.

"Calm down miss! Show us where this is taking place.", an officer replied.

Nikki jumped back into Mark's car and the police followed her back to Thomas' house. "Thank you, Lord, for helping me to get some help so fast. Nikki prayed, while on her way back to help her mama. Finally, they pulled back into the driveway of Thomas' house. I jumped out, oh my God, I think my soul left my body when I saw my mother laying on the ground covered in her own blood.

"Sir, you need to drop your weapon! PUT THE KNIFE DOWN, NOW!" The officer told David. Daddy then began to stab himself multiple times.

"No! Somebody, please stop him! Why God? Please don't take my father away!", I prayed

Sadness invaded my worlds and it seemed as if everything around us had stopped. A feeling, that no words can describe, came over me when they covered mama up with a white sheet. Everything was taken from me at that moment. I was in shock and numb. "This cannot be happening. This can't be real." Was what kept going through my mind, over and over. I wouldn't wish that kind of pain on my worst enemy. The pain was so thick I felt like it was going to suffocate and kill me. I didn't know what to do.

Stripped Away

Later that morning, the rest of the family met up at the hospital. Daddy had stabbed mama twenty-six times and daddy died on the way to the hospital. The ultimate sacrifice had been paid. The pain had become unbearable for us all. We were now motherless and fatherless children. David stripped eight people of what was so precious to them.

Everybody that were there the night of the incident had to be questioned. Afterward, everyone was free to go. When we returned home, everything felt so empty and lonely without mama. Everybody was just going through the motions. We were here physically, but not mentally or emotionally. We all had to take it second by second because the pain of our loss was so heavy, and it was the hardest thing that we would ever endure. The light that brightened everybody's world was no longer there. I can't even tell you how we made it, but somehow and some way everyone managed to pull together and go through, so that mama could be put away with a nice service. All the family met up at the house to talk about what all needed to be done.

Mama's oldest brother was a pastor, so he did the preaching at the funeral himself. He was able to assist us in many ways. Zack was really upset about the way he had to lose his sister. He held his self together though, because he knew he had to handle pretty much everything. His sister's eight kids wasn't in the shape to handle anything.

It's Saturday, 2:00 p.m. and the church is slam packed! "Oh God, you know best, and we choose to trust you in spite of!" Zack said, as he mourned over his beloved sister, Susan. Nikki sat in a daze not really in tune to what is taking place around her. She had become numb to life itself and all she could think about was that her beautiful queen and best friend had been taken from her.

"Oh, he killed my sister!" Annetta cried out like she had done lost her mind. The day of the funeral was really heartbreaking, and it had been the type of event a person would never forget. Everyone said their goodbyes and fair wells, in hopes that it all was only a dream. Not even a week of mama being put to rest, people that said that they would be there slowly began to disappear. Having to give up mama's house had been a really hard decision for us, but it had to be done because we weren't able to maintain the bills.

Eve was the oldest, so she agreed to let her other siblings come and live with her. The grass isn't always greener on the other side. Eve began to be mean to Nikki and her other brothers. After the death of Susan, a lot of things changed in the family. No one was so close as they used to be. For some reason or another people treated the four youngest differently, because David had been our father. As if we had a choice of who our father had been. Over time things got a lot worse. It was as if it had been two separate families and we had to fend for ourselves.

"Bitch! Get out of my house, right now!" Eve yelled" You are the reason Mama is dead in the first place!" She screamed at Nikki.

"I can't believe she feels that way about me." I thought. "Wasn't family supposed to be there for one another." I said to myself, as the tears fell down none stop.

I went to see mama that night. I wept from the bottom of my soul and couldn't stop. "I didn't think anything like this would happen." I mumbled to myself. From that day on, Nikki isolated herself from the world. "Lord, I have a child I have to live for. I know that I can't give up and I need you to give me the strength to make it. Please, help me." Nikki prayed to the Lord. She just remembering the times her mother taught her to fall down on her knees and pray. Just sitting and thinking about the good times she had with her mother, brought a little life back into her.

"Baby when life tares you down you are in the right position, because then you're on your knees, and you can pray. Nikki remembered her mother saying that to her. That day a steel little voice spoke to her and told her to keep pushing and not give up.

It's been a month since mama was buried. "Mama, I miss you." I said to myself. I was wondering, how the world could still go on when a queen is no longer inside of it. "It was time for me to boss up and start getting my life in order somehow." Nikki said. "Eve, will you watch Qarnontae until I get off work, please" Nikki asked.

"Yes. He can stay until you get off and by the way, I would like to say I'm sorry about what I said to you." Eve said.

"MA!" Qarnontae called, as I was leaving out the door.

"Yes, Qarnontae, what is it?" I asked my son. "I'm hungry." He said.

"What do you mean? Haven't you eaten something today?" "No ma'am."

"What?! I am gonna make you something to eat really quick before I go. Come on."

Later I found out that my child had went an entire day without anything to eat. Talk about mad, I was beyond pissed the fuck off! Now, it's to the point that I have to stand for me and my child, no matter what the cost may be. I was about to turn eighteen in a few weeks, so I had to make it do what it do. I was able to get Qamontae inside of a daycare while I worked. I wasn't gonna have my child being neglected any more. Now I could work in peace.

"How may I help you?" The lady at the front desk asked.

"I would like to fill out an application for an apartment, please." I told her. Things went as planned on that day and all the papers had been filled out correctly. By the grace of God, I was placed at the top of the waiting list for the next opening. It's Thanksgiving Day and it's the first holiday without mama so ain't nothing going on. It's really a dreary day and nothing is the same since she has been gone. We are all lost.
"Things are just all fucked up now without mama." J-dog said to Knot, while sitting on the porch. Knot, reassured J-dog, that they will get through it. "Thanks bro. I needed to hear what
you had to say." They <lapped one another up and fired up a loud blunt. It's now 1:30 a.m.

"No, no, no! Somebody please help me!" Nikki jumped straight up out up the bed. Hitta came running in to see what was going on.

"Are you okay, Nikki?" He asked her. "Yes, I'm fine. What's wrong with you?" Nikki asked him" I just had another nightmare."

"It's okay, Hitta. Everything is alright, so go back to bed. We have a really long day tomorrow." Nikki said. It's another day and it's stormy outside. The entire day supposed to be like this and I'm not able to see anything out this car window. Eve carefully pulls into the daycare to drop Qamontae of and her next stop will be to drop Nikki off at work. NO matter what the sister still wanted to get along because all they really had was one another. Nikki kissed Qarnontae, when she got him inside the daycare.
"I love you, mama." He said, giving me the biggest hug ever

"I love you too son," Nikki said. As I was headed into work, many things began to invade my thoughts. I'm doing whatever I can to make it for me and my family, the best way that I can. The struggles of life had me stressed out. I felt like no matter what I did it wasn't enough. I felt like we would never catch a break.
"Be still and know that I'll fight your battles for you. Lay your burdens at my feet and take my yoke because it is easy. I heard a still small voice say to me. Walking in the door of Zaxby's, my boss, Ms. Jones, stopped me right as I walked in.
"Can you please step into my office?" She asked Nikki. I had not even clocked in for work yet. What now? I thought, while stepping in her office, to see what it is she could want. "Well, I'm

sorry to have to do this, but I'm laying you off for two weeks."
She told me.
"WHAT?!" I snapped at her. Why?" I asked.

"Because you have been showing up late three days out of a week lately and that type of behavior will not be tolerated around here, no exceptions. Look Nikki, you're a very good worker and that's why I am not firing you, but I need you to take this time to decide if you really want this job -I-have no choice. You're free to go and I-will see you-back here in two weeks." With that being said she turned and started doing her paperwork and I was standing there looking dumb founded. Storming out I was pissed the fuck off! Hell, I could only get here when I had a ride. I be damn! IF it ain't one thing it's another. I didn't know what my next move was, but I had to figure something out. I called Eve to see if she would swing by and pick me back up. Of course, she did.

CHAPTER TWELVE

I had been sitting in the backyard, under the big oak tree, that sat in my sister's yard. I sat there for about two hours, thinking and getting my thoughts together. "What's wrong, Nikki?" Knot asked.

"I'm good little bro, just thinking about things and life, that's all." I told him. "So, what's up with you, not? What's been going on with you lately?"

"Nothing much, sis. Just been cooling it, nothing new going on. Same old bullshit, just a different day. One thing's for show, I miss the fuck out of mama, Nikki." Knot didn't like to show any type of emotion, so he pushed off before the tears came. I could tell that he was in his feelings. "I got to go Nikki. I'll catch up with you later."

"For show." I told him. We clapped each other up and Knot took off. After Knot got gone, my brother-in-law started in with his bullshit. "GET YOUR NASTY HANDS OFF ME!" I yelled at him.

"Shhhh!" He whispered. I jumped up and ran into the house because I just knew somebody would be in there and he wouldn't be able to fuck with me. I was NOT in the mood for his nasty ass. I was wrong though cause nobody else was there. DAMN!

"You can't run now, can you?" He said. I desperately wanted somebody to come home so they could save me. Damn, I wish I would have asked Knot to stay with me for a while. It was no one there, but me and him. He started kissing me on my neck and the shit started feeling good.

My pussy got wet, and I was getting weak, so finally I got tired of fighting and thought, what the hell. I was like, why not use what I got, to get what I want. Shit, it's a dog-eat-dog world and I had to do something to take care of me and my son. I entered into a world of betrayal that day and I did it by any means necessary. He was one nasty nigga because he ate my pussy and my asshole, like he was a starving man. He paid me real good just to let him taste me and taste me he did. He wasn't shit, just like every other man in the world and that's why I think I was leaning more toward liking women. I was still confused about that though. Men will make you want to be gay.

Months has gone by and I was no longer working. Things wasn't looking good on my end and one way or another, I had to get some money. Selling pussy had become my new profession and boy, was I good at it. I was making the money, but I kept my focus, so I wasn't letting the money make me. Shit, the next thing I knew I was in my own low-income apartment, that I had paid for months in advance. One of the things that was in agreement, with me and my family, was for me to go back to school and get my GED. Hell, my rent was only seven dollars a month. Shit, you couldn't beat that deal, it was the best deal ever. So, I just kept doing what I had to do to keep a roof over me and my child's head. In the apartment complex it seems as if every hood bitch lived in that area. The first few nights in my new spot was hell. Knot ad J-dog came rushing into my spot, as if they were running from the pigs.

"What's up?" I asked them. J-dog had slammed the door and was telling somebody to go the fuck on.

"Lame ass nigga's!" J-dog yelled.

"What's going on?" Nikki asked them again.

"Man, sis, these niggas were trying to jump us!" Knot said to me. "Yo sis, call Hitta and Tray. Tell them I said pull up because there is a situation that we need to handle ASAP!" I did what he told me to and the next thing we heard was BOOM! BOOM! BOOM! A loud thump is all you could hear, coming from the other side of the door. The noise was so loud, if the apartment wasn't made out of bricks, whoever the nigga was would kicked the entire door down. That's how hard it sounded. The phone started ringing and Hitta picked up on the second ring.

"What's good sis?" He asked, from the other end of the line.

"Look bro, we got a situation over here at my spot. Circa said. Hitta, we need you and Tray to pull up, so we can handle it."

Before I finished talking Hitta was loading his burner and putting it in his waist, he handed Tray the other weapon and they in less than twenty minutes. It was time to put in some work and take care of the nigga who was fucking with my brothers. I was still on the phone with Hitta stnd he told me to put something behind the door. He also told me to have J-dog and Knot, go out the back and meet them at the top of the hill. Pulling up on whatever Hitta was already busting, not caring who got hit and he cleared the entire block. After that night, shit fell in place like it was supposed to and I ain't have no more problems. They found out quickly that we are extremely close. One thing for sure, when the Jones boys showed up, they shut the whole city down! When it comes to fucking with them niggas the streets had second thoughts. If you didn't know, you would quickly find out!

We Will Get Through It

Months later, the younger boys, J-dog and Knot, was sent out of state to do a bid on some burglary charges. Since mama had been gone, things was slowly doing downhill. J-dog would call us to let us know that him and Knot was in the same institution. He assured us that they were good, but we kept them straight too with commissary.

I'm finally back at work and since I had to get something quick, I accepted a position at the Waffle House. Seemed like I was back where I started, but it is what it is, for right now.

"Hey yo, Nikki!" One of my co-workers yelled.

Oh shit, it's one of my homeboys from across the way. "What's good, Tyson?" Tyson liked men, so me and him got along really well. We started hanging out a lot after work.

"Nothing. Shit, what are you doing after work?" He asked me

"Ain't nothing going on, what's up? What you trying to do?" I asked Tyson.

"Well, I wanted to know if you would ride with me tonight, to this party. It's supposed to be off the hook, but I don't want to go by myself. You down with it?"
"Hell yeah! I'll pull up with you." I told him.

"It's on then!" Tyson said, with a smile. "I'll pick you up around ten o'clock, so be ready!"

"I got you." I told him, while laughing at his crazy ass. After clocking out from a busy day, Uncle Luke was playing, "PUMP, PUMP, YO, GET IT, SHAKE SHAKE SHAKE A LITTLE SOMETHING, THAT'S THE WAY, YEA THAT'S THE WAY, YOU GONE GIRL!"
When me and Tyson hit the party, ass was everywhere, all over the place!

"This joint is live as FUCK!" Tyson screamed over the music, that was flowing from the DJ booth. "I'M ABOUT TO CATCH ME ONE HONEY!!" Tyson yelled, while popping his ass. He could do the damn thing better than any female in the joint! I love him cause he sure does how to party! I was laughing my ass off at him. I was about to bust a nut laughing at his crazy ass!
"Man Tyson, I ain't had this much fun in a long time!" Nikki said.

"Stick with me and that's all you will ever have is fun!" HE said. Tyson was straight giving it to them ran and uncut. He was getting his dance on, for real and vibing with the music.

"Tyson! Tyson!" He finally heard me over the music.

"What's up?" He asked me. "You are fucking up my groove!" "I can't stay out too late. I got to be leaving soon." I told him.
"That's cool girl. I got you." He said, before hitting the floor again.

"Shit I'm about to get me some juice so I can get a little loose." I said to myself. I damn sure wouldn't talking about no apple juice. I wanted me some Gin and juice! I knew I couldn't drink too much though, because I had to make sure Qamontae, got on the bus in the morning. Besides, my niece be thinking she grown, so I wouldn't be surprised when I get home that she has her little boyfriend in my house. If she does, I got something for her ass, for real.

"Alright, all the sexy ladies!!!" The DJ started. "Let's get this part started right! Let's start by playing a game of spin the bottle." DJ Slick hollered into the mic. The crowd went wild! Tyson and I were having a blast!

"Come on, girl! Let's get in the game. We came to have some fun, not stand around looking crazy." Tyson said, while he was pulling me in the direction of where it was about to go down.
"Calling out our first two contestants!" I just be damn! He called me out with some nigga name Nard. I know Tyson must have set this shit up, but I played the game anyway. What the hell. We partied so hard I barely remember that night. One thing for sure.

Tyson made sure I got home safe. 6:00 a.m. BUZZ! BUZZ! BUZZ! I rolled over to shut the alarm clock off.

"Oh shit!" Nard jumped up and so did Circa. They both looked at each other in total confusion.

"How did we end up in my bed?!" Nikki asked Nard. "Just calm down little mama." Nard said

"No nigga, you calm down! I don't just bring no nigga to my spot like it's all good.

That's not how I rock!" Nikki said.

"Well, we must have drunk too much at the joint last night." He said. After that night, I couldn't keep Nard away. We started kicking it on the regular. At first, dating Nard wasn't that bad. Shit, it seemed as if we were only living in the moment sometimes. For some reason or another, I found myself drinking a lot more then I would.

"Hey Hitta!" I was excited to see my big bro walk through the door of my job. "What's up? What brings you this way on a nice Monday morning?"

"Well Nikki, I really need to talk to you." He told me.

"Okay cool. Give me just a minute. Have a seat and I'll fix you a cup of coffee while you wait, okay?"
"Okay, thanks." Hitta told Nikki. A few minutes later, Nikki walked over to the table where Hitta was sitting.

"So, what's good bro? What you need to talk to me about?" I asked him.

"Well Nikki, you know what J-dog gets out in a week, so will it be okay for him to come stay with you, for a little while? Until we can figure something else out." Hitta said.
"That's cool. Besides, I need a babysitter while I'm at work, so that would help me out a lot. My niece just needs to go anyway, because I can't handle that shit with her ass anymore. She has all types of niggas in my shit when I'm at work." Nikki said. Hitta, was really in his feeling today and Nikki could tell it.

"I know something else is going on with you. I can feel it, so what is the matter?"

"I just be really missing mama like crazy, Nikki."

"I know Hitta. Believe me, I know how you feel." Then I repeated what mama used to say all the time, "We will get through it." Then, I gave him a big bear hug before he left.

When I got off work I went home and when I walked into my apartment I was caught by surprise.
"You little bitch!" A hard hit went straight upside my head! It almost caused me to lose my balance. I stumbled a little trying to catch myself from hitting the floor. "You nasty bitch!!" Is all I could hear Nard say. He hit me again with another blow to the head. He beat me like I had stolen something from him!

Breaking my arm in six places! He beat me like I was a damn man in the streets! "You listen to me and you to me well, Nikki! I run this shit! Don't get yourself fucked up." Then, Nard turned around and walked out the front door to the apartment, as if nothing ever happened. I just bawled up on the floor and cried my eyes out. Nobody should have to come home to this, especially after working hard all day. I was in so much pain that I couldn't even pull myself together enough to go into my bedroom.

Calling the police wasn't an option, so I had to load my face up with make-up, to cover up the two black eyes Nard had given me. I just couldn't understand why he beat me the way that he did. First, I had to watch my dad beat my mom all my life. Now the man that I have beats me.

This was a curse, and I cried my soul out. Qamontae came rushing in the door from school. I hadn't even realized it was time for him to come home, I was so distraught.

"Mama, are you okay?" He asked me.

"Yeah baby. I'm okay." I told him the lie, as I quickly pulled myself together. The last thing I wanted was for my child to see me that way. I didn't want him to be exposed to none of the unhealthy things that me and my siblings seen when we were growing up. I wanted things to be as normal as they could be for him. After that I day I never really saw Nard as much. I was putting in as many hours-as I could to stay away from him. "I got

106

something for Nard's ass." Nikki thought. This shit has to stop, and I mean that.

CHAPTER THIRTEEN

Over the next few weeks, things between me and Nard had gotten really bad. DFACS showed up at the apartment, because they received complaints.

"Good morning Ms. Jones." The case worker, Mr. Loudermilk, greeted me.

"How can I help you, ma'am? It's seven in the morning and I was still in the bed." I told her.

"Well Ms. Jones, I'm here about some reports of violence in the home. I understand that you have a son by the name of Qamontae, right? Whenever there's a child in the house it's my job to come out to see if the allegations are true. Before I knew it, I slammed the door in the lady's face.

"What the fuck." I whispered to myself, while standing on the other side of the door.

KNOCK, KNOCK, KNOCK.

"Ms. Jones, I'm not going anywhere, so you need to open the door. Let's go ahead and face whatever is going on. Maybe I can help you." Ms. Loudermilk said.

"GO AWAY!!!" I yelled at the door. Knock, knock.

"Ma'am, if you don't open the door and talk to me, I will be forced to call the law."

"Damn" Is all I could say, before opening the door and allowing her to come in. "Mama, I miss you." I whispered while looking up at the ceiling. I was mad as hell! "How dare this man come into my home and try to destroy it." I thought to myself.

After a short meeting with the caseworker, she informed me that the case would stay open for ninety days, one home visit per month. "I have to stay on my shit." I said to myself, after she walked out. "For some reason or another, I can't seem to get my life together." I was telling Tyson over the phone."

"Everything will work itself out for the best. You just have to hang in there, Nikki." Tyson said, before ending the call.

"SURPRISE!!!!! WELCOME HOME LIL **BRO!!!!!**" The apartment was slam packed with people. They were all there to welcome J-dog home. The grill was already fired up, music was playing, and everybody was having a good time. We were caught off guard when the sound of something being knocked over, came from inside of the house. We all rushed from the back yard, into the house. When we got in there, the first thing we seen was, Nard and J-dog fighting.

"You pussy ass nigga! Don't you ever put your hands on my sister again!" J-dog was yelling. Every blow that made contact to Nard's face caused major damage. Nard had no fight against my brother. The sound of his jawbone cracking was heard while J-dog was beating his ass.

"Don't you never, whop, again, whop!" J-dog was talking to Nard while he was beating him down. "Please! Stop J-dog!" Nikki called out. "Please stop before you kill him! You just got out! I don't need for you to fuck your life up again! I need you here, so this won't happen!" Nikki pleaded for Nard's life to be spared. We finally got J-dog and pulled him off Nard. J-dog walked back outside like nothing happened, grabbed a cup of Ciroc and turned it up. Nard chose not to stay after that.

"I'm outta here!" Nard said. As he was walking away, he looked in Nikki's direction, with a kiss my ass look on his face and flipped her a bird.

"Yah, that was a damn good fight! That shit might have turned me on. Now, let's get back to the party bitches!" Tyson said. We all bust out laughing at his crazy ass. One thing for sure, Tyson knew how to party and he had the entire hood lit up, from the food he was burning on the grill. We had every meat you could think to name on the grill. From pork chops to chicken wings. Everybody partied hard that day and we all had a ball.

"Do you know what, Tyson?" Nikki asked him.

"No, I don't know until you tell me." He was being funny like always.

"Anyways, I am tired of Nard's ass and him always fucking up." Nikki told her friend. "It's really time for me to get away from his low life ass, Tyson."

"Girl, I know bitch. Nard ain't shit and h ain't helping you do shit. Hell, you are barely making it yourself. Anyway, one of your fine ass brothers is gonna end up killing his ass if you keep fucking around with him.

"I know, Tyson. Look I need to-tell you something, that I haven't told anybody."

"What's up Nikki? You know that you can tell me anything." Talking to Tyson was so easy for **Nikki.**

"Well, I am pregnant by Nard. I can't believe he ain't beat it out of me yet with all the fighting we do."

"You're what? Bitch, did I hear what I thought I just heard, Nikki?" Tyson was in shock.

"Yes, you did, Tyson." Nikki wasn't happy about it at all. "Yeah, I'm good. I feel a little uneasy that's all." The only thing J-dog had on his mind was to reach his destination, so he would be-able-to handle his business. He was headed to get what belonged to him, no question asked. The rest of the ride was quiet. The only word spoken was, J-dog telling Tray, to pull up to the apartment 225. J-dog jumped from the car, once it was in park. Reaching the door of 225, it was already open.

"What the hell!!!" he said Something isn't right about this. One thing for sure, J-dog stayed ready for the bullshit. As he remembered what had been told to him many times, if I stay ready, I don't have to get ready, pulling his strap from his waist band J-dog approached the apartment. He pushed the door open just a little bit more, slowly not causing any type of noise. That same uneasy feeling seemed to creep back inside of his belly. As soon as he entered the front door, Tank drew down on him.

"What's up, fuck boy?" Tank laughed. "I see you slipping, huh?" He was holding his .45 at J-dog's head. J-dog didn't show any type of fear at all, and Tank was the one slipping on his shit, not noticing the nine J-dog held in his right hand, case the apartment didn't have much light. Without a second though, he popped Tank in his left foot, causing a lot of pain.

"Naw fuck boy, you got caught slipping nigga." J-dog said, while walking in the direction of Tank's safe. When he got it unlocked, he cleared that shit out. On his way to exit, he finished Tank off. "No body, no witness, no murder." J-dog said, as he was walking out of the apartment. He got back in the car as if nothing happened. Tray knew not to as any questions, so he just drove off without a word. J-dog was not to be fucked with and that's just the way it was.

CHAPTER FOURTEEN

Nikki was standing on the hill by the basketball court. "Excuse me ma'am, do you know a Nikki Jones?" The officer asked her. "You damn fool." I thought to myself. I told him that I was who they were looking for. Reading me my rights, the officer placed cuffs on me and put me in the car. Off to the county jail I went. I was standing in front of the jailer, listening to my charges.

"Ms. Jones, you are being charged with aggravated assault and attempted murder." The

C.O. told me. When I heard my charges, I blacked out. I woke up in a cold cell. A bond was set a week later.

"Ms. Jones, you are not to have any type of contact with your victim. Do you understand me?" The judge asked me.

"Yes, your honor. I understand." Hitta posted my bond, and all my brother's was in the parking lot waiting on me. All of them except Gain. Being set free on a ten-thousand-dollar bond was the best feeling eve. Jumping back out into society I stayed focused and didn't give Nard a second though. It was late one night later on in the week, and I hear a hard knock on my front door. I went to see who it might be. I know I wasn't expecting anyone this time of night. "Who is it?" I yelled at the door.

"It's me man. It's Nard. Let a nigga in."

"Hell naw! You trying to set me up! I was ordered by the judge, to stay away from you. No, I can't let you in." He refused to leave, and we went back and forth, for about 10 minutes. I was feeling confused, I opened the door. "I need you God. Please help me." I mumbled to myself, sending a silent prayer above. I let him in in hopes that I wasn't making the wrong choice. From that day on we acted like everything was okay. I always kept a house full of shit for my lil brothers. We were back at my spot. Knot and J-dog didn't want to follow any of my rules. They had become so off the chain kicking in people doors and shit. They were out of control, and I couldn't do anything with them, I could barely do anything with myself.

Boom! Boom! Is all you heard when the door flew open. Ms. Grant went running across the floor. "Lay the fuck down!" J-dog demanded. Mr. Mrs. Grant didn't reply immediately, because Mr. Grant was a feisty old man. Knot came down on his face with his 9mm, giving him two quick blows back-to-back. You could hear his jawbone crack, with every blow, as Knot made contract. "I said lay the fuck down old man." Mr. Grant complied. Knot and J-dog were the type of niggas that bared none.

Back at it again and Nikki was back to drinking heavy. She delivered her second child. Everything was moving so fast, and things were a lot more difficult. "All I ever wanted was a normal life." I thought to myself. "What the hell is normal." I began to question. Nothing seemed to make sense to me anymore. While sitting at the head of mama tombstone, tears fell from my eyes, non-stop. I couldn't stop the tears from falling. I couldn't understand why it hurt so bad. At this point in my life, I felt like fuck the world and fuck the people that live in. Shit became very reckless that day. Months later DFACS pulled up at my front door and snatched my kids away from me. Shit most definitely started going downhill. I lost my apartment a week later.

My aunt Lisa wanted my daughter, but she didn't want my son. If I could choose, I would have had my two kids in one house, but I didn't have say at this point. DFACS had taken that from me, and everybody had become a suspect. I started fucking people up right and left, not really giving a fuck about the aftermath. If I felt like you were in violation with me or did something to me, I was fucking you up, case closed/ Pushing Luke's brand-new Camaro down 75, I was headed to a house party I was invited to. I have the music turned all the way to the max. I have my drink in the cup holder ad I'm sipping as I ride. One of TI's songs is playing and I'm vibing to the best. "Nigga try to play me I'm gonna blow them off the map asap, asap, asap." I was feeling every word that he was speaking through the system.

I was on some bullshit that night and on my way to the party. Riding the gas pedal, not giving it any mercy at all. I'm doing 75 in a 55 zone. I dropped my cigarettes on the floor, I bend down to reach for it and before I knew I lost control of the car, going off the road. I hit something on the roadway, causing me to flip the car six times. I thought I had died, and I guess God wasn't ready for me just yet. Pulling through, reality kicked in. "I have to get out of here fast before the police come!" I thought. I climbed out the back window that was already busted and took off on foot. I later blacked out from all the blood I lost, and I woke up being detained. I was taken down to the county jail. I wanted to hurry up and be booked before they realized I was out on bond already. I was hit with all type of charges that night. Thank God a bail was set, and I was able to sign myself out.

Pulling up, back at home, I smelled nothing but loud in the air. I knew my brother and them was in there blazed up. I couldn't get in the door fast enough. They kept a good blunt rolled. We smoked so much that night we could barely see each other the thick cloud of smoke that lingered in the air.

"Hey yo, sis!" J-rock yelled out. "Pour me up a drink before you come back." We smoked and drank until we passed out on the couch. We were all awakened in the middle of the night from a loud knock on the front door. Knock, knock, "Police department, open up!" It seemed like we had just closed our eyes. I rolled over to check and see what time it was. "What the fuck." Is all I could think. I wanted to know what the police was doing at my door this time of morning. I was only in this two-bedroom house temporarily.

I sat on the couch, just waiting to see what would take place, next. Lord, please don't let them find him I prayed. .--

"Alright, you guys." I heard Sgt. say about fifteen minutes after starting the search. Let's get out of here." They left.

"YES!" I said, in a low tone, as they were leaving out the front door.

"If you see him tell him to come by the station." Sgt. Wishbourne said.

"Hell, J-dog knows y'all looking for him." I said. Then I slammed the door hard behind his ass.

"Damn did, that was close." Is all J-dog could say and we laughed about it while firing up the loud.
"Pull over!" Oh, shit another burn to his right arm.

"Shut up!" I told Ben before I knew it burned his ass again with the lit cigarette I was smoking while joy riding in his car. "Didn't I tell you to sit your ass back?" Shhhhh another burn on his arm. Every time put the cigarette to his skin you could hear the flesh burn and smell it too. "I'll give you your car back when I'm ready." I told him, pushing his Chevy. Ben had an old school Chevy, and I tricked his ass out of his car. Thinking he was about to get some ass. That's what his nasty ass gets. Every time I thought of him trying to come on to me, I stuck the cigarette to his ass.
"Ahhhh! Please stop burning me!" I plan to let him know who was in charge one way or another. I didn't give a damn about nothing at all. Fuck feelings, is how I felt about it. Ben was drunk, so I had the upper hand, in the situation that he was in. Pulling to the side of the road, I got dressed and headed to see what the pigs wanted, this time. As I was walking to the door, I said to myself, "It seems like everywhere we go we seem to draw the police."
J-dog stopped me in my tracks and told me they may be looking for him. Boom! Boom!

"Open the door! It's the police department!" They repeated again. No time to give it a thought J-dog climbed in the refrigerator. I opened up to let the pigs in.

"So, what's up?" I asked Sergeant Wishbourne.

"Well, well, well. Where if your brother, with that squeaky voice." He asked.

"I don't know where he is Sgt. I haven't seen him in months and hell, it might have been a little longer than a month." I said.

"Well, Nikki, we still need to search and see if he's hiding here." "DAMN!" I whispered. "I hope they don't find him."

Shaking me from my thought Sgt. Wishbourne said, "Now do you know if he's in here you're going to jail too for lying to us."

"Whatever," I told him. Hell, I wasn't giving my brother up. They would have to do their jobs today.

"Alright, you guys, let's search the premises." Sgt. told his crew of four other officers. I took all his money, before leaving him and his car in a wooded area. I really didn't have any remorse. Hell, life didn't have any for me. DFACS wasn't cutting me any slack when it came the most important two people in my life. Shit, the way things are going I may be looking at prison time. "Don't you say a word, Tyson. Give me what you got in the cash register. I told him. Why the fuck am I'm robbing my job. Fuck it" I thought.

"What are you doing?", Tyson stated with confusion.

"Listen, just do what I ask, because I don't want to do anything tonight that I will regret.

Hurry up Tyson! I don't have time to talk!" Yelling at my close friend. He did what he was told, pocketing about $650.00 before I turned to walk out. Luke was waiting in the car for me. I got in and he pulled off. "You know what it is." I told him as I looked at him and smiled. It was time to get high, no questioned asked. Spending a few hours with Luke.

I was ready to hang out, so I got him to dropped me off in the hood.

"Say, Doug."

"What it do Nikki?" as we dapped one another.

"What's up fella?" Nikki asked.

"Shit nothing much, lil ma what you up to?" he asked. "Just cooling on my high."

"Oh yeah? Let a nigga get down." Doug said.

"Yeah, but I got to go get some more from my house." I told him. "My aunt only lives a block from the hood, so I'm headed to snatch up her ride." I did remember that she never takes her keys out her car. I didn't give a damn about nothing at this point. The only thing I wanted was another hit. "Just like I thought." I said to myself, once I noticed the keys was in the car. I jumped in and headed to pick up me a couple sacks. "Hell, my aunt won't know I'm in her car." I told myself. Headed back after picking up my work, I noticed that a cop car had been trailing me. I didn't know my aunt reported her car stolen shortly after I pulled out her driveway. Here I go again, being housed in the county jail and being booked on stolen vehicle charges. God was indeed on my side. I was able to bail out again that night.

Finally, visitation had been approved for me to visit my baby at the DFACS office. I was happy that I was able to visit at least twice a week. Grabbing and holding my babies meant the world to me. When I had them in my arms, nothing else mattered, only them. "Mama, I'm ready to come home." Qamontae said. Every time he would tell me that it broke my heart in pieces.

"I know baby. I'm ready for you to come home too." I told him, while holding him close to me. The hardest part was having to leave them; I can't believe my sister wouldn't help me with my kids. IT seems as if no one cares, for real. I wept that day uncontrollably. The tears that fell from my eyes wouldn't stop even if I wanted them to. I cried myself to sleep that night.

Months had passed by, and I still hadn't gotten my kids back. Over time I slowly lost them to the system. After that nothing else in life mattered. It's just the way I felt. Partying and drugs was my escape from life.

"WATCH YOURSELF! Some balled headed bitch had the nerve to tell me. Before I knew it I was off in her shit. I was not to be fucked with and I was a walking time bomb, case closed! Falling down on my knees early one morning I prayed that God would hear me. "Lord I need you in my life." At that moment, I knew it couldn't be no one   , because I heard a still voice say, "Trust in the Lord your God with all your heart and lean not to your own understanding." That sounded very familiar. It came to me that it was the same thing Rev Walker talked about when I was young; the day mama took all of us to church. "Yes. I said to myself.

Thank you Lord. My life still hasn't changed and I thought that something would've been

different, but it wasn't. I have to swallow my pride and call Eve. She answered on the second ring.

"Hello, what's up Nikki?"

"Listen sis, I know that we haven't been on the best terms, but I would like to say I'm sorry. If I haven't never needed you before, Eve, I need you now. Please help me." Nikki said. "I don't have anywhere to stay, can I crash on your couch until I figure something out?"

"Alright Nikki, you have six months." We agreed and hung the phone up. Not even two weeks after moving in with my sister I received a letter from superior courts, letting me know that I had a court date coming soon. "Shit, I might have to go up state. How will my story end?

CHAPTER FIFTEEN

My story isn't uncommon, especially for many people who grew up witnessing dysfunction as a child. Many children are raised in traumatic situations and that lead to generational cycles of abuse, neglect, and bouts with the foster care and justice system.

My goal as the author of this story is to help others who were raised in dysfunction, regain control over their lives, and rewrite their story. This book is the first of many tools that I will create and use to serve others in the foster care and justice system. Like Nikki, you too may know what it's like to be caught in a cycle of violence and dysfunction that seems to have no end. Stay tuned for the next release about Nikki's story.